Sweet Lips

Tennessee

Sweet Lips

Tennessee

A NOVEL

Dani Lou

Green Tulip

GREEN TULIP PUBLISHING
Published by Green Tulip Publishing
USA

For more information about the author, please contact:
Green Tulip Publishing
greentulippub@gmail.com

Or
Visit:
www.greentulippub.tumblr.com

ISBN-10:   0-615-89306-6
ISBN-13   978-0-615-89306-8

Revised April 2014

PRINTED IN THE UNITED STATES OF AMERICA

To my parents, my greatest inspirations

In loving memory of my grandmother

ACKNOWLEDGEMENTS

To my parents, thank you for years of faith, love and encouragement, as I pursued this endeavor and many more. I'm grateful for the many sacrifices you've made, your prayers and constant support in my life. Thanks for the shoulders I often cried on and the hours of conversations we had, as I worked towards the next phase in my life. I love you both!

To my brother, I love you more than you know. I'm proud of who you're becoming and can't wait to see where life takes you! Keep persevering and know, I will be cheering for you at the finish line!

A special thanks to Dr. John Friedl, my professor, supporter and friend. No matter how grim opportunities proved and despite the devastation, after many doors were slammed, you always encouraged me to push for more. Thank You!

To Mrs. Sue, thank you for your willingness to spread God's word. When I need them most, your prayers and support are always there. Your life is a testament that God loves His people and always takes care of them. Thank you for your walk with Him!

A heartfelt thank you to Ms. Thompson. "Blest are the meek: for they will inherit the earth." Your compassion and support of my family is profound and you have a heart of gold! I love you!

Thank you to Mr. Johnson, for all your support and kindness. You're an awesome person, with a big heart. You have a Word from God and it serves as a blessing to anyone who listens.

2

Thank you for the prophetic words spoken over my life. They're coming to pass!

To Mrs. Dianna, my supporter and friend, thank you for the prayers and spiritual endowment. God always sends you at the right times. I appreciate every piece of literature, scripture, and prayer you send my way. They're greatly valued and so are you. I love you much!

Thank you to Aunt Gayle, one of my biggest supporters. Your support and kindness is greatly cherished. It is a genuine support and one that is valued beyond measure! Thanks so much for your love and warm spirit. I love you to pieces!

To Mr. Williams, thanks for your prayers and support. I appreciate the encouragement over the years, as I sought out to persevere and work towards a brighter future. It means so much!

To Mrs. Elizabeth, thank you for the unadulterated truth. No sugar coating, or watered-down advice, just pure honesty, with sprinkles of love. LOL! Thanks so much, I love you!

To The Pitts Family, thank you for the prayers and support. I appreciate your thoughtfulness and constant outpouring of love. I love you all!!

Hola, Mrs. Daniels. You've been here from the beginning. Not only has your encouragement motivated me, to keep persevering, but your ambition to tackle your own dreams, serves as a guide for me to want more. Thank you for the prayers and support. Love you much!

A special thanks to Mrs. Millie Tyler, for your support and unyielding kindness. It's comforting to still have a teacher, after all these years, who lends a kind word, accompanied by a smile. Thank You!!

Thank you to the Code & Foster families, for your love and support. Our kinship is age-old and it's a blessing to still have supportive friends, after all these years. Thanks so much!!

To Ms. Carole, a sincere thanks for your encouragement and genuine love. On some of the roughest days, you always seemed to keep me smiling. I love you!

To Coach Brooks, thank you for your constant support through the years. In moments of celebration and times of fellowship, I could always count on you to be there. Thanks again!

Thank you to Mr. and Mrs. Adams for the love, encouragement and support. In times of laughter and hours of confusion, God used you both to pray and encourage my family, and we can't thank you enough!

To Ms. Princess and family, thanks so much for the love and outstretched arms. It's comforting to have friends, I regard as family, outside of home. Thanks for everything! XOXO.

To Sgt. Earl Monroe, thank you for the impact and difference you made upon my life. I value your input and concern for my future. Even to date, I exercise those core values of Integrity First, Service before Self and Excellence in All I Do, and I can't thank you enough for your leadership!

To Ms. Champion, thank you for the warm welcome. Your extended hands lightened the burden and made my journey a little bit easier. Thanks again, it meant so much!

To Ms. Jones, thanks so much for all your support through the years. I can attest that under your leadership, I gained a strong sense of professionalism, integrity and character and I can't thank you enough for the opportunity!

To Mr. Bowman, thank you for your friendship and support. Your prayers and encouragement are always timely and uplifting, and mean so much. Thank You!

Thank you to Mr. and Mrs. Greg Bowles for the prayers, encouragement and love shown. You're believers, who operate in the truth and I'm proud to call you my friends!

To Ms. Combs, thank you for your support after all these years. The next time, I'm in your neck of the woods, I'll definitely drop by!

Lastly, a special thanks to the woman who remained committed to her passion for teaching. To Mrs. Ronda Foster, my English teacher, who pushed for excellence and caused me to fall in love with writing, THANK YOU!

Thanks to all my family, friends, teachers, professors, coaches, co-workers, supervisors, neighbors, supporters and encouragers for your kindness. I appreciate all the prayers, support, laughs, fellowship, camaraderie, messages and calls over the years. From the friendly smile, from the bank teller and kind word from the cashier, at the grocery store, you all helped in shaping who I am today. THANK YOU!

Rain splatters on the kitchen window. Mae Ruth looks up and notices water dripping from a soiled patch in the ceiling.

"Shit!"

She jumps up from the table and quickly runs over to the cabinet. She grabs a pot and places it on the floor.

Mae begins humming to herself. As she sits back down at the table, struggling to feed an agitated toddler, Quincy Sr. storms in the door. Drenched in rainwater, Quincy slams down in a chair. His face filled with much frustration, he hits the table and Mae jumps from her seat.

"Damnit Mae," he begins. "I'm sick of it. I been pullin' them long shifts, down at the factory and it's all in vain. I come to work early and show them white folks I'mma hard worker and they still don't give a damn. Me and Danny Mack know that section better than any white boy in there and they still made William Argyle lead crewmen over our line." He looks down at the supper on the table.

"I can't freely feed my family or earn a decent wage," he continues. "A Right to Life, Liberty and

Happiness[1] HELL! My life ain't right, my liberty ain't won and my happiness ain't happened."

"Quincy," Mae interjects, "I know you angry, but fussing ain't gone change nothing. Baby, we both been working hard, to make ends meet and that counts for something. Jessie even said I could earn extra money, working some nights at the club." Quincy leans back in the chair and laughs.

"Mae," he says. "Baby, them people down at Jessie's ain't goin' nowhere. They so busy mixin' they dreams down the barrel, of a *Joe Black* bottle, and the train[2] done already passed 'em by." He reaches over and holds her arm.

"Baby," he continues, "them white boys is playin' on the stock market, while we sittin' round playin' butter and egg.[3]" Quincy lifts from the table and stands at the counter.

"I want more," he says. "More for my family." He drops his head, staring down at the aged sink. Mae leans down and kisses her bouncy boy.

"We getting by," she replies. "We gone make it." She holds up the baby, as he smiles in mid air.

---

[1] Lines from the United States Declaration of Independence of 1776.

[2] Opportunity.

[3] An illegal numbers game.

Quincy Sr. remains silent and angrily stares out the kitchen window.

The following morning, a rooster sounds outside. Mae yawns and stretches from a night's rest. She notices the fan, loudly buzzing in the corner, but yielding no air. She shakes her head in disappointment.

Mae rolls over and shuffles the cover, in search of Quincy Sr. Noticing the light, shinning from the hallway, she calls out for him.

"Quincy…Quincy baby, I know yesterday was rough, but we gone make it. Baby?"

She raises from the bed and journeys down the hall, to the bathroom. Pushing the door open, she sees a letter fastened to the mirror. Curious, she retrieves the paper and silently reads:

Dear Mae:

I've left headed north. I hate to leave you and Junior behind, but I'm losing myself, in a foreign land. I must go where I can be recognized as a man, a black man who matters. This ain't the end, but the beginning to something big and when I'm settled, I'll send for you and the boy. I love you and Junior and right now my leaving is for the best.

-Quincy

8

Mae drops to the floor. Hanging onto the sink, she heavily sobs.

"Noooo….no Quincy!" she exclaims. Screams are heard from the other room, as Quincy Jr. cries from his crib. Still sobbing, Mae leaves the bathroom and walks across the hall. She lifts the baby from his bed, holding him close to her chest.

"We gone make it," she says. "We gone make it."

1973

Outside, music blares from Mae's kitchen window. As she washes dishes, taps are heard on the front door. Humming to herself, Mae and Quincy Jr. retreat to living room. Visible in the doorway, is Claudeen Draper, Mae's neighborhood friend, known for loosely parading around the community and sipping *Joe Black's* dark whiskey.

"I didn't think you was gone eva answer that doe," says Claudeen. Mae opens the door and beckons for her to come inside. Claudeen looks down at Quincy Jr., who is smiling in the doorway.

"Hey Q," calls Claudeen. "Look at you. Grinning from ear to ear and growing like a weed."[4] Claudeen looks back up at Mae.

"Damn Mae Ruth," she continues. "And look at you. Quincy done left and you done gone and took a sip of the devil's nectar. Mrs. Henrietta would turn in her grave, if she knew you was down at Jessie's, serving up whiskey to them sinners." Clearing off the counter, Mae swings around.

"You one to talk," she says. "Last week you was spooning wit Charles Matthews and when that didn't work out, you started cuttin' up wit Flip Turner."

"Well," replies Claudeen. "Charles was quite the lover, but his money wadn't right. Never had nothin' to contribute. Broke as Joe's damn turkey.[5] And Flip, girl that boy's a dream chaser. Ain't worth a dime. Ain't got a pot to piss in or a window to throw it out of[6], but wanna leave and chase some five dollar dream." Claudeen shrugs her shoulders.

"That's why I commits to none," she says. "It's better that way. Let him do his business and by mornin', get the hell out my house. No staying for

---

[4] A growth spurt.
[5] Impoverished.
[6] Financially unfit.

cigarettes or coffee. It's for the best. Just do his business and leave." Mae shakes her head and laughs.

"Well, it's nothing," she begins. "I'm just down at Jessie's to earn some extra money, for me and Q, and one day leave this tied town behind." Claudeen looks back at her.

"Whatever you say Mae Ruth," she says. "But you know, you ain't goin' no where and I ain't neither."

Claudeen and Mae lift from the couch. They head outside, where they are met by Rosalee Harris, who is sitting at the far end of the porch. With an attitude, Claudeen slams down in a chair and abruptly greets Rosalee.

"ROSE!" snaps Claudeen. Rosalee sternly looks up.

"CLAUDEEN," mocks Rosalee.

Claudeen looks off, staring back into the street, as Mae takes a seat beside her.

"Can't you two be civil?" questions Mae.

Mae rests back on the chair, rubbing her hands. Rosalee looks over, at Mae's swollen fingers and shakes her head.

"Mae Ruth," says Rosalee, "you better let somebody look at them hands of yours. You'll be

11

somewhere broke down, foolin' wit[7] Clara Lewis and them damn linens, and it'll be business as usual for her. That white woman a be gone on, bout her business, and you'll be somewhere all mangled up and hungry. That's what's wrong wit black folk now. We don't take care of ourselves and pay[8] for it later. And by then, we got the gout, high blood pressure, Arthur[9] and everythang else."

They are interrupted by screams heard across the road. Claudeen stands up on the porch. Ahead, she sees Carrie Richardson kneeling on a step, fastening her son's coat. Carrie soothes the boy's face.

"Now James," says Carrie, "momma has to go, but I'm comin' back. Nana gone take real good care of you. She gone rear you right. And when I'm settled, I'm comin' back for you."

Carrie turns to Eva, who is seen rocking in a chair.

"Momma," she continues. "I appreciate this and when I'm settled, I'll come back for him." Eva grabs her arm.

---

[7] To associate with.
[8] Suffer.
[9] An acronym for arthritis.

"Carrie," says Eva. "You just remember one thing: A boy should always be able to count on his momma, even in a world grim and grey." Nodding her head, Carrie quickly turns to exit.

"Ok momma," she calls. "I love yall and I'll be back real soon." But as she turns to leave, Eva calls back from the chair.

"And Carrie," she says. "A momma who fails her boy, has already failed at life itself." Now anxious to leave, Carrie quickly nods and climbs into the cab. As she waves from the window, the cab pulls off. Eva consoles the sobbing boy and ushers him inside.

Claudeen motions to leave the porch, and Rosalee speaks from her chair.

"That's a damn shame," calls Rosalee. "Poe boy ain't gotta chance." She looks over to Mae.

"You know, it used to be a time when kids could always count on they mommas. Tuh, oh how times have changed." She begins rocking in the chair.

"Momma's baby, daddy's maybe?[10] Honey, that girl don't give a hoot[11] bout that boy and nobody else." Rosalee shakes her head with disgust.

---

[10] Stereotype of a mother's ever-present role in a child's life, while the father's input is often uncertain.
[11] To be carefree.

"It's like fightin' a losin' battle,"[12] she continues. "That girl gone do what she wanna do anyway. Up behind some slick,[13] that'll get her another one for Eva to raise." Rosalee nods in the chair.

"It's sad honey," she continues. "That girl done took the butter from the duck.[14] Runnin' round wit every Tom, Dick and Harry and Eva left scramblin' to pick up the pieces."[15] Rosalee shakes her head.

"Every time some smooth talker come along, she do Eva like this. Promise her, she gone do right and come back for them kids. And time and time again, don't nuttin' be done changed. Eva let her come back and she do the same thang." Rosalee turns up her lips and throws her hand.

"Honey," she says. "You can only lead 'em to the brook, but you can't make 'em drank it."[16]

Reaching the yard, Claudeen calls from below.

"See," she says, "that's why I commits to none. It's only for the best. No burdens for momma and no headaches for me." She winks at Mae, but Rosalee shouts back from the porch.

---

[12] A pointless matter or inevitable situation.
[13] Sly talking man.
[14] Exhaust all resources. To take the best of someone.
[15] To struggle to financially provide for one's self and or family.
[16] Term which suggests that change lies with individual.

14

"You right about that Claudeen," says Rosalee. "No headaches for you or your momma…Just the man's wife." Claudeen looks over and rolls her eyes, but Rosalee continues speaking.

"Now Claudeen," she says. "Ain't no need in you pitchin' no hissy fit."[17] She looks at Mae and throws her hand.

"That child looser than a goose,"[18] says Rosalee. She rears back in her chair and laughs uncontrollably.

Claudeen abruptly swings around and angrily stumps off up the road. Smiling, Mae shakes her head and returns back inside.

Mae calls for Quincy from the kitchen.

"Quincy, Quincy baby get up. I'm gone be late for work." She scrubs the kitchen counter.

"I've got to head over and finish up laundry for the Lewis' and you know how they get about being late."

"Shoot," she says.

---

[17] Throw a tantrum.
[18] A sexually promiscuous person.

She cuts off the eye, on the stove, right before the kitchen begins to smoke. The crisp bacon sizzles in the skillet. She opens a window and fans the air. Plopping down at the table, she calls out to Quincy.

"You'll only be over to Eva's, a short while. Jessie asked me to help her tonight, at the lounge. When I'm finished, I'll be right over to get you."

Mae and Quincy leave the house and head over to Eva's. While walking, they encounter Willie Lampkin, Otis, Slim and Mr. Jenkins, who are standing in front of the store. Mr. Jenkins calls out to them from the steps.

"Hey Quincy, my boy," he says. "How's that pitch of yours?" Quincy Jr. bashfully smiles.

"It's going…" he begins, but Mae interrupts him.

"It's going," she says. "I don't mind Quincy and his ball playing, but he's got to get an education." Mae looks over to Willie and rolls her eyes. She grabs Quincy, by the hand and they proceed towards Eva's.

Willie Lampkin enters the street and calls out to her.

"All that boy need is somebody to teach him a firm grip and them white folks' a be handing out contracts in no time." Otis and Slim laugh from the store. Smirking, Mae swings around.

"A firm grip?" she questions. And I suppose you got one?" Willie cunningly smiles back.

"Yeah baby," he says. "I'm quite the teacher." Mae rolls her eyes.

"Well," she continues. "Quincy has plenty of time for learning ball, but for now, it's all about his books. Good Day." She strolls off, with Quincy and they head for Eva's.

Otis, Slim and Willie admire her figure from behind. Holding a tooth pick in his mouth, Willie shakes his head.

"Ooh wee," he says. "Girl know the Lawd been very good to her."

Otis and Slim reply back in unison,

"Yesss indeed."

They laugh on from the store, as Mr. Jenkins shakes his head.

2

Outdoors, Quincy and the neighborhood kids are playing in the street. James Richardson, skipping rocks, encourages Quincy to join in.

"Hey Q," he says. "I bet you can't throw like this?" James skips a rock down the dusty road.

"Yes I can," replies Quincy. "I'm gone pitch for the Giants, when I get -big."

"You?" replies James. "Pitch for the Giants? They ain't gone let no black person, from Sweet Lips, play no pro-ball." Quincy aggressively stares back.

"Uh huh," he says. "My momma said when my daddy send for us, it's gone be a lot we black folks can do up north." James throws his hand in annoyance.

"Man whatever," he calls. "Hey Q, let's play a game." Quincy nervously inches back.

"Man no," he replies. "The last time I played that game with you, my momma whooped my tale off." James laughs uncontrollably.

"It'll be different this time," he says.

"How?" asks Quincy. James flashes a devious grin.

"This time," he says, "we gone play at Mrs. Hazel's house." Quincy takes another step backwards.

"NO way!" he belts. "Slim and Otis said she skins them goats, in her backyard and eats 'em. They said she eats people too." James shakes head.

"Awl man," he replies. "You know them fools a say anythang. But I bet Willie McCovey[19] would do it." Quincy looks back at Hazel's house.

"Ok ok," he says. "I'll go. But you have to come with me."

"Deal," says James and they both shake hands.

They both arrive at Hazel's house. Quincy timidly lifts the lever and walks through the gate. He looks back at James, hesitant to move.

James frowns from the street and points to the house. But remembering his infamous spanking, Quincy ponders whether he should ring the bell. He takes a deep breath and walks up the worn steps.

But stooping beside the picket fence, James yells to him from the street.

"Go on and ring the bell, or are you scared?"

---

[19] Former African American baseball player and San Francisco Giants first baseman.

Quincy moves closer towards the door. As he lifts his finger to the bell, the door swings open. In the doorway, six foot four, wrinkly and aged, stands Hazel Roberts, with a meat cleaver in her hand.

In shock, Quincy screams and runs for the street. But forgetting to lift the latch on the gate, he hops the fence and cuts his knee.

"Ahhhh," he screams. He brushes past James and heads for home. Laughing in the road, James calls for Quincy, who is barely visible in the dust.

"Q, wait up," shouts James.

Hazel wickedly grins from the porch. Slamming the door, she returns inside.

Quincy bolts into house, nearly knocking Mae to the floor.

"Quincy!" she yells. "What have I told you bout runnin' in this house? And what happened to your leg?"

"Momma," begins Quincy, "James dared me to ring the bell, but before I could, she opened the door with a cleaver. So I ran."

"Quincy," continues Mae. "I told you to stay away from Hazel, them damn goats and other folks' dinner tables." She sits down at the table.

"If it's one thang momma taught me, it was to mind my own business, help those who can't help themselves and don't be eatin' any and everybody's food." Reminiscing, she lights a cigarette.

Seconds later, James is seen bent over and panting from the screen. Mae stirs from her chair and leans forward.

"James," she calls. "James is that you?" Terrified, James faintly calls out from the porch.

"Yes Ma'am," he mutters.

"Boy," calls Mae. "Quit standing there, suckin' your teeth. Come on in here." James smiles from the screen and enters the house.

"Don't be lookin' all scared," says Mae. "Quincy told me what happened. Come on over here."

James sheepishly maneuvers over to the table. With the cigarette, hanging from her mouth, Mae rubs the suave on Quincy's knee. She looks over to James.

"You ate today?" she asks.

21

"Yes ma'am," he says. "A biscuit and grits, this morning." Sighing, Mae shakes her head and puts out the cigarette.

"Well," she continues, "you gone eat with us tonight. You and Quincy gone and wash up." Quincy and James retreat to the bathroom, in the hall. Clearing off the table, Mae calls out to them from the kitchen.

"James, how your nana and sister doing?" Giggling and playing in the sink, James gives a delayed response.

"Um…they doing good," he says. Mae nods her head.

"That's good," she says. "How your brother Benny? He still in South Carolina?"

The room remains still. James doesn't answer. He and Quincy are heard laughing uncontrollably and throwing water.

"QUINCY!" Mae bellows. "Boy if I have to come in there…Wash up and come in here and eat!" Quincy and James continue laughing and return to the kitchen.

Taking his seat, Quincy quickly picks up his fork and begins eating. Mae ruffles in her chair.

"Quincy! Boy, have some respect for the Lord. You know we say Grace first, what's wrong wit you?" She rolls her eyes.

"Now hold hands," she says, "bow your heads and close your eyes.

"Dear Lord, thank You Heavenly Father for this day. Lord, thank You for health, love, family and James..."

James peaks open his eyes. But catching a glimpse of Mae, he quickly shuts them. Mae smiles to him, from across the table.

"...Lord," she continues, *"thank You for him being a guest in our home. Lord Bless these boys, their future and wherever you may take 'em. And Lord, let this meal be a blessing to our bodies for Christ's sake, Amen."*

In unison they all say Amen.

James picks up his fork, preparing to devour the soulful meal, but stops.

Quincy looks up from his plate.

"James you gone eat, cause if not, I will?" Mae interrupts him.

"Boy hush." She turns to James.

"James," she continues. "Baby, why you not eating your food?" James drops his head.

"Well," he begins. "I just ain't had this kinda eatin' since my papa died." Mae sadly smiles.

"Well," she says. "Eat up and you can take the rest home to your nana and sister."

Rubbing her knees, Mae smiles and lifts from the chair. As she turns, headed for the bedroom, Quincy calls to her from the table.

"Hey momma," he says, heavily chewing. "You leaving?" Mae turns around.

"Yeah baby," she calls. "I'mma go take a little nap. James you finish up and get on home and get that food to Eva, you hear?" Mae turns and heads for the room.

James looks over to Quincy and bows his head. Quincy looks over at the colored television, in the living room and calls back to Mae.

"Hey momma," he says. Mae turns around once more.

"Yeah baby."

"Can me and James watch *My Favorite Martians?*[20]" he asks. Mae smiles and looks down at James.

---

[20] A popular cartoon series from the 1970s.

"Yeah baby, but when it's over, James you hurry home and give Eva that food." Tilting his chin forward, James bashfully nods.

"Yes ma'am," he mumbles.

3

As lightning flickers over Sweet Lips, Mae tosses in her sleep.

"No...no no," she cries. She rolls over and continues sleeping through the dream.

1961

From the dream, young Mae Williams walks into the dining room and kisses her mother on the cheek.

"Hey Momma," she says. Henrietta glances up and smiles.

"Hey baby," says Henrietta. "After we pick up the dresses for the choir, we're heading over to Janie's to see bought Darlene." Mae frowns.

"Momma," she says. "What's wrong?" Henrietta shakes her head.

"I don't know baby," she says, "but something's telling me to go up there."

Mae and Henrietta arrive to Janie's, where cars are straddled up the drive way and alongside the house. Puzzled, Henrietta parks the car. She steps out, where people are seen huddled together on the porch. Henrietta hesitates, but Mae climbs the steps.

Janie greets them at the door.

"She passed," says Janie. "Mae, Darlene passed." Confused, the message doesn't register. Janie begins to weep.

"Mae," continues Janie, "Darlene passed. It was the fever." Mae pauses.

The words ring.

"Passed!"

Mae covers her mouth and begins to scream. Clasping her hands, Janie looks down in silence. Henrietta begins to cry uncontrollably. Observing the guests, about the porch, Mae gathers herself and maneuvers past them. Frustrated and angry, she sprints to Darlene's room. Still sobbing, Henrietta follows behind her.

Inside the room, Mae stands beside Darlene's bed. She looks down at what appears to be a sleeping girl. Gently rubbing her cheek, Mae looks over to Henrietta, who is weeping at the foot of the bed.

Mae turns to leave the room. Looking straight ahead, she walks outside to the car. Henrietta hugs the others around the porch and heads for the car. Mae remains silent looking out the window, as Henrietta slowly pulls off.

As Henrietta continues up the road, she begins to scream. Dropping her head, she loses control of the wheel.

"MOMMA!" Mae yells. "Momma watch out!" Henrietta looks up and grabs the steering wheel, barely missing the pole. Loud screeches are heard and thunder sounds, awaking Mae from the dream.

Mae stirs from the bed. Sweating profusely and disoriented, she calls out for Quincy Jr.

"Q...Q baby, what are you doing?" Holding her head, she enters the living room.

"Quincy...Quincy!" she calls. Mae shakes her head and attempts to straighten up. Peering into the kitchen, she notices Eva's supper still on the table. She picks up the gently wrapped plate, to walk it over.

Outside, the sky is dark and the wind is heavy. Mae pushes down her gown, as it blows in the wind. Reaching Eva's porch, she knocks on the door.

"Hey, Mae baby," answers Eva. "How you doing?" Mae looks away.

"I'm doing alright," she says.

"Yeah," says Eva. "That's always good to hear. You know, your momma woulda been proud of you. The way you're committed to the church, working and rearing Quincy right." Mae scratches her head and looks down in shame.

"Yeah," she says. But sensing her guilt, Eva transitions to another subject.

"Speakin' of that boy, where is he?"

"I don't know," replies Mae. "He and James were eating supper, when I laid down. I told them that after that show went off, to bring over this food." She holds up the plate.

"Well thank you baby," continues Eva. "Times been rough and I try to make sure he gets plenty to eat. Him and his sister. You know Carrie left me with 'em." Eva shakes her head. Mae nods and looks back down at the porch.

"Yeah," she sighs. "I know…"

They look out into the street, where lightning flashes across the sky. Mae pushes down her dress, struggling to keep her balance.

"Well Mrs. Eva," she says. "I'mma head on and try to find Quincy." As she journeys down the steps, Eva calls out from the screen.

29

"Ok baby," she says. "And if you see James, please tell him to hurry on home." Mae looks back and shakes her head.

"Yes ma'am."

Mae motions to enter the street, and is nearly swept away in the wind. Witnessing the sight from the general store, Mr. Jenkins calls out to her in the street.

"Mae," he says. "Girl, you better get on home. Looks like we bout to get a good one." Mae nods and calls back to him.

"Yes Sir, I know," she says. "But I can't find Quincy. Have you seen him?" Puzzled, he shakes his head no.

Mae nods and heads up the road. As she disappears in the wind, Mr. Jenkins returns inside the store.

Mae walks about the community looking for Quincy.

"Q, Q baby," she calls. "Where are you?" Distraught, she becomes consumed by the wind. Nearly falling, she grabs a hold of a pole in the street. Now overwhelmed, she begins to sob.

Sprinting in the distance, James is seen running from the woods. Heavily breathing and barely audible, he calls out to her.

"I…I think he got 'em," he says.

"Got who?" Mae frantically inquires. "James, where is Quincy?" Terrified, he attempts to speak.

"He…he…he got 'em," James continues. Mae becomes agitated and begins to shake him.

"Who got him?" she commands. "Where is he?"

"See," continues James, "we was walking in the woods and saw Hollywood's shack. I told Q Mrs. Mae, I promise I did. I told him we should leave." James looks down at the ground.

"But he said we should make up for the dare at Mrs. Hazel's house. So, he went up the steps and knocked and Hollywood opened the door." Mae becomes antsy and continues to shake him.

"What happened James?" she questions. "What happened to him?" James begins to cry.

"We ran, but he kept chasing us. I told Q to hurry up and he was behind me. We kept running and I could see the store up ahead. But when I looked back, they were gone." James continues crying. Now hysterical, Mae sobs uncontrollably.

The townspeople begin to pour into the street. Irate and exhausted, Mae heads for her house. Claudeen calls out to her from the street.

"Mae…Mae calm down. Mae where you going?"

Mae storms out the house, with a butcher knife. Brushing past the crowd, she heads for Hollywood's shack. The townspeople stare in awe. Claudeen follows closely behind her, as she continues up the road. Slim looks over to Otis.

"Man," he begins, "You know that fool Hollywood's crazy. Greeted the church ladies, last Christmas with his daddy's old pistol." As Mae whist past them, Slim and Otis beckon for Mr. Jenkins and Willie to follow her.

Mae reaches Hollywood's shack and bams on the door.

"Hollywood," she says, "you son of a bitch. Where's my boy? You bring him out." Mae continues beating on the door.

Hollywood surfaces to the screen, as Mae continues yelling.

"You son of a bitch," she continues. "I know you chased them boys. Where is my son?"

Hollywood Massengile, the town misfit, who drew to the outskirts, years ago, steps out onto the porch.

"I…I…I Hollywood Massengile," he begins. "Momma named Sue Massengile. You wanna come inside?" Dressed in blue shorts and a tan overcoat, Hollywood eyes the curious pack around his porch.

Mae's anger intensifies. Desperate, she begins beating him in the chest. Confused, Hollywood flinches and covers his head.

Mae sinks down on the porch and begins to sob.

"You got my boy," she continues. She looks out into the crowd, where Slim, Otis and Willie are seen running from the woods.

"He got my boy," she calls. Willie pulls Mae away from the porch and attempts to comfort her.

"I know, I know," he says. "We gone find him. Come on." He ushers her down the steps.

Hollywood gathers himself.

"You…You not gone stay to color pictures?" he asks. Heading back for town, Willie turns and shakes his head.

"No Hollywood," he replies. "Not this time." Willie grabs Mae, by the hand, and she continues sobbing up the trail.

Over the next few weeks, the people of Sweet Lips band together, in search of Quincy Jr. Mr. Jenkins supplies goods from the store, as the townspeople cover ground near the woods. Ulla Nixon's boys travel 50 miles south, to spread the word to the residents of Monroe County.

One morning, Claudeen drops by, to check in on Mae. From the street, she notices Mae rocking in a chair on the porch. Her appearance is unsettling, clothes soiled and her hair hasn't been combed in days. Claudeen approaches the porch, holding her breath, to avoid the stench.

"Hey Mae," she says. "I brought you some biscuits. Momma made 'em this morning." Claudeen puts the basket on the steps and looks back out into the street.

"…Pretty day out," she continues. "Yep, a great day to sit out and enjoy this sun." Mae looks out into the street and continues rocking in the chair. She mumbles under her breath.

"I'm his momma," she begins. Tears begin to flow.

"I promised to protect him, love him and give him all he needs. Keep him safe. And I let him down." Claudeen begins to cry. She walks over to console Mae.

Ahead, Otis, Slim and Willie are seen dashing up the road. As they reach the porch, Slim runs up the steps.

"Mrs. Mae," he says. "We was there all morning, looking for him. We was gonna keep looking, but we found this."

He reaches over and hands Mae one of Quincy's sneakers. Mae looks down at the shoe and bursts into tears. She takes the shoe and holds it close to her chest. She nods in appreciation. Claudeen leans over and rubs her shoulder.

"Don't worry bout it Mrs. Mae," continues Slim. "Lord willin' and the creek don't rise, we gone find him. Just keep praying." Otis reaches into his pocket and frowns.

Willie stands at the bottom of the porch, with a tooth pick in his mouth. Sympathetically, yet cunningly, he looks up at her. Mae flashes a slight smile and continues to sob. Across the street, Eva stands in the doorway and drops her head.

Claudeen jumps to her feet. She shoos Slim and the others into the yard. From the street, Slim calls back.

"Mrs. Mae," he continues. "You just rest up. We gone find Jr." With tears still flowing, Mae humbly nods.

Willie turns from the road and chimes in.

"Yes ma'am," he begins. "We gone find him. Just get some rest." Mae remains silent.

"Ok?" continues Willie. Mae looks out into the road and smiles.

The three men head up the road, leaving Claudeen and Mae on the porch. Relieved, Claudeen begins to speak.

"Now Mae Ruth," says Claudeen. "I didn't think you was eva gone smile. The Lord does work in mysterious ways[21]." Mae smiles and bows her head.

"And while He's in the working business," continues Claudeen, "maybe, just maybe, He'll give me strength to get you cleaned up and do something to that head of yours." Claudeen helps Mae from the chair and they go into the house.

---

[21] References Isaiah 45:15 (NLT).

4

Pearson's Pointe

A week later, Quincy's body is found at the bank of Pearson's Pointe. Jimmy Shipley, one of Mr. Chamberlain's crewmen, discovers the body, while relieving himself in the bushes. Later that evening, Claudeen assists Mae, in making funeral arrangements and schedules for services to be held, on Sunday, at the Sweet Joy Baptist Church.

Sunday-Funeral

Outside the church, Mae is dazed and delirious. She waits outside, with Claudeen, tightly gripping Quincy's sneaker to her chest. The ushers open the doors.

Ahead, Reverend Thomas is surrounded by several lilac flowers. As the organ begins to sound, at the podium, Reverend Thomas is heard reciting John 14:

> *"Let not your heart be troubled: ye believe in God, believe also in me..."*[22]

---

[22] References John 14:1, KJV.

The pallbearers enter the church, with Quincy's body. Following behind, Slim and Otis escort Mae to a pew.

Mae scans the church. To her left is Mother Wilson, who is humbly smiling to her below. As Mae proceeds down the aisle, whaling and screams ring from the rear of the sanctuary. Exhausted, Mae approaches the pew and takes her seat. Close friends and distant relatives, follow suite and fill in the remaining spaces. Rev. Thomas continues from the pulpit:

"I go to prepare a place for you. And if I go and prepare a place for you, I will come again, and receive you unto myself; that where I am, there ye may be also."[23]

As he finishes up the scripture, Deacon Jones enters the pulpit. The choir stands to its feet. Deacon Jones clears his throat:

"Through the years, I keep on toiling,
Lord I'm toiling, through storm and rain…"[24]

Displaying a faint smile, Mae closes her eyes and reminisces back to 1956, a Sunday at Sweet Joy Baptist Church, where she and Darlene first met.

Sweet Joy Baptist Church- 1956

---

[23] References John 14:3, KJV.
[24] Lyrics to popular gospel song, *When the Gates Swing Open.*

From the dream, Minister Allen is heard singing before the congregation:

> "...*Patient, patiently waiting and watching,*
> *Until the SAVIOR, comes again,*
> *Hide, me in your love..."*

The church is small and the air is murky. Church fans are waving and the congregation is heard shouting and clapping their hands.

Darlene Johnson is seated in between her parents. Mae Ruth, positioned on the pew ahead, turns around and flashes a shiny smile. As she waves to Darlene, from the above, her mother nudges for her to turn around.

The congregation begins to stir and raises from the pews. Minister Allen continues from the pulpit:

> "...*And when it's over, Write my, my name above,*
> *Hey hey, when*
> *The gates, swing open,*
> *I'll, walk in..."*

He continues.

> *"Teach me..."*

Agitated and anxious, Mae turns back around, where Darlene is still smiling on the pew. She bends down from the seat and beckons for Darlene on the floor.

40

Surprised but bored, Darlene crawls on the floor. Below, both girls lie facing each other.

"What's your name?" asks Mae.

"Darlene Johnson," responds Darlene. Mae examines the girl's bouncing curls.

"I like your hair, you got a perm?" she asks.

"No," replies Darlene. "It's pressed."

"Oh," responds Mae. Mae scans the floor.

"Look at all this stuff under here," she says. Under the pew, the girls spot loose change, boxes of tissue, a bobby pin and an earring.

"I'm 7," continues Mae. "How old are you?"

"I'm eight," says Darlene, "but my birthday's in January." Mae looks around the church.

"Oh," she says. "Is it always noisy in here?"

"Pretty much," replies Darlene. "My momma said Minister Allen takes forever to end a song." The girls giggle on the floor.

"Do you wanna be friends?" asks Darlene.

"Ok," says Mae, smiling. "But, we have to shake on it."

The girls shake hands and continuing laughing below.

"We'll always be friends," says Darlene. "I'll never leave you."

41

Mae snaps back from the dream. Ahead, Reverend Thomas is heard giving closing remarks.

"...*And He'll never leave you, nor forsake you. Amen.*"[25] Tears stream down Mae's face. The congregation stands to its feet. They sing a hymn and go out.[26]

The following morning is quiet. Outdoors, few townspeople are visible and Mae keeps to herself. Barely eating, she avoids public interaction and spends much of her time in her bedroom.

Later that night, Mae struggles to sleep. Tossing and turning, she is consumed by a lurid dream.

1955

From the dream, Mae Ruth is seen standing in the screen door, in the living room.

"Mae Ruth," calls Henrietta. "You better get from in front of that door. It's lightening." But humored, Mae continues looking from the screen. She

---

[25] References Hebrews 13:5 NIV.
[26] References Mark 14:26; Matthew 26:30.

is taken by the site of Raymond and Diane Little, who are fussing on their front porch.

"RAYMONDDDD!" bellows Diane. "I done told you to get them clothes, off that line. Now, its finna rain and they gone get wet again."

"Awl woman," he replies. "Don't nobody wanna hear your mess, this early in the mornin."

"RAYMOND, RAYMOND!" shouts Diane. "You heard what I said. I ain't washin' them clothes again." Diane returns inside and slams the door.

Raymond throws his hand and sits down in a chair on the porch. He lifts a bottle from underneath a table and begins drinking.

"I shoulda listen to my momma, when she told me bout you the first time," calls Diane, from inside. "She said you wadn't no damn good and she knew you couldn't keep a job!"

"Awl woman," replies Raymond. "Hush up." He takes another sip from the bottle.

"All you do," she continues. "Either at Jessie's, in some heffa's[27] face, or down at Dale's, borrowin' money and tellin' damn lies." Still watching, Mae laughs from the screen.

---

[27] A southern derogatory term for an unsavory woman. The exact term is heifer, which references a young cow.

Taking another sip, Raymond lifts from the chair. As he proceeds down the steps, into the yard, Diane calls again from inside.

"I tell you one thang," she begins, "I ain't gone worry bout it, no damn more. It'll be your ass that ain't got nothin' to wear tomorrow." Raymond throws his hand and begins removing garments from the line, as lightening continues striking over Sweet Lips.

Henrietta looks into the living room and notices Mae still standing in the doorway.

"Ok Mae Ruth," she calls. "You gone get struck by lightening." She shakes her head and walks back into the kitchen. Mae continues standing in the door and observes Raymond in the yard.

"Woman gets on my damn nerves," he mutters. As Raymond reaches for another pin, lightening flickers and knocks him to the ground.

Still watching, Mae gasps from the screen, as Diane bolts out the house. She looks around and notices Raymond twitching in the yard.

"Oh naw you don't, you lazy fool," she says. "Playin' possum.[28] You ain't gone get out of it this time. Get up Raymond, get up." A foamy substance

_____

[28] To act or play dead.

begins seeping from Raymond's mouth. His eyes begin to roll. Panicking, Diane screams for help.

"Help, somebody help!" she yells. People begin pouring into the street, as others are seen sprinting up the road.

Mae remains stock-still at the door, gazing at the lifeless body, under the clothes line. Thunder sounds and she twitches, waking her from the dream.

5

Mae raises from the bed and wipes her face. For nearly three weeks, she has remained in house, still distraught from Quincy's death.

She journeys over to the window and looks out. In view, Eva is seen kneeling and picking collards from her garden. Mae pauses. She walks into the living room and opens the front door. Startled by the noise, Eva looks up. Sighing, Mae walks over to meet her.

Outdoors, the atmosphere is steamy. Locals are seen about their yards and lollygagging[29] in the street. Mae awkwardly walks over to Eva, who is now stringing beans on the porch.

"What yall doing?" Mae asks. Eva looks up with ease.

"Oh, nothin' baby," she says. "Just tryna to get ready for supper tonight." Mae pauses and chuckles.

---

[29] Gossiping or chattering.

"Well," she says, "the rate you goin' it'll be all night." Eva giggles in relief. Mae sits down, beside Eva and begins stringing beans.

Awakened by the commotion outdoors, James appears in the screen. Facing forward, Mae calls out to him from the porch.

"Boy, I see you," she says. "Ain't nobody ever told you I got eyes in the back of my head?" Mae nudges Eva, who humbly laughs, beside her.

James remains frozen in the doorway. Mae looks back at the screen and beckons for him to come outside. Tense and terrified, James opens the door.

He draws near Eva, fearful of Mae's reaction. But sensing his guilt, Mae wipes her eyes and continues stringing the beans. James glances down at her and attempts to speak.

"Uh…Mrs. Mae," he says.

"Yeah baby," she answers, tears streaming down her face.

"I'm sorry bout Quincy," he continues.
Mae pulls her last string and covers her face. She begins sobbing uncontrollably. James stands motionless on the porch.

"I know baby, it wadn't your fault," she says. "Quincy is in a better place, you know." Mae leans over and hugs him tight.

"…He's wit the Lord now," she says.

They all look out, as the sun begins to come up over Sweet Lips.

6

1976

Mae removes the apron, from her waist. As she prepares to sit down, at the kitchen table, taps are heard on the front door. She walks over to the screen, where she is greeted by a bubbly Claudeen Draper.

"Mae Rue," says Claudeen. "Do you ever wear anythang else, besides that Judy on Duty getup?"[30] Mae glances over and rolls her eyes.

"But not your kind of Judy,"[31] she says. Claudeen winks at her from the door.

"Claudeen," Mae continues, "what do you want?"

"Well," says Claudeen, "you can start by letting me come in." Mae opens the door and they both walk into the living room. Sitting on the couch, Claudeen begins pouring in the day's gossip.

"Have I got news for you," she says. Mae shakes her head.

---

[30] Cleaning attire or apparel.
[31] A hooker or promiscuous woman.

"Girl," continues Claudeen, "Jessie said Willie Lampkin's back in town. Say he pulled up to Jenkins' Store, in a Cadillac and was all decked out.[32] Say he been to New York City." Mae rolls her eyes.

"She said he had some other fellas with him too," Claudeen continues. "Important lookin' men, and they'll all be at Jessie's tonight."

Now folding clothes, from a laundry bin on the floor, Mae nods in sarcasm.

"Claudeen, that's real nice," she says.

"Nice?" questions Claudeen. "Mae Rue, it's more than nice. It's an opportunity of a lifetime." Mae rears back on the couch and laughs.

"Opportunity?" she says. "Child please. Willie Lampkin is nothing but trouble." She lifts the basket from the floor.

"Claudeen," she continues, "the man rolls up, draped in two years worth of rent, driving round in my pension and retirement and that don't seem odd to you?" Claudeen yanks a towel from Mae's hand.

"Mae," she begins, "you been working steady and ain't been out the house, since Q died. Let's go to

_____

[32] Nicely dressed.

Jessie's tonight. Willie told her everythang's on the house."

"Claudeen," Mae responds, "I'm not for sale." Claudeen falls to the floor.

"Wit all them men watching," she says. "I couldn't dare go out by myself. Mae, oh Mae please? I need you to come with me."

"Ok, ok," says Mae. "I'll go, but you better behave tonight. And I can't stay long. Some of us have work in the morning." Claudeen winks at her and heads for the door. But before exiting, she calls from the doorway.

"And Mae," Claudeen continues, "please don't wear that apron." Laughing, Mae lifts from the couch and pushes Claudeen out the door.

"Bye Claudeen," she says.

As she turns to head back inside, she is greeted by Rosalee, who has been listening on the porch.

"Hi you, Mae Ruth?" asks Rosalee. Looking straight ahead, Mae responds back.

"Fine Rosalee," she says. But in sarcasm, Rosalee calls back to her.

"Uh huh."

Mae faintly smiles and attempts to return back inside. As she turns, Rosalee continues speaking from the porch.

"Mae Ruth," she says. "Where you headed tonight?"

"Oh, nowhere in particular," says Mae. "Just down to Jessie's, with Claudeen. They having a little get together[33] tonight." Rosalee begins rocking in the chair.

"Uh huh," she says, pointing. "Child, you better stay way from that Claudeen Draper. That girl is looser than a nail in that picket fence."[34]

Laughing, Mae turns around from the screen.

"Honey, I'm serious," says Rosalee. "That girl ain't got no cooth.[35] Ain't worth the salt in her bread[36] or the hairs on my chin. Mae calls back to her from the door.

"She alright Rosalee."

Rosalee shakes her head and turns around in the chair.

"Shiiiit," she continues. "Margaret Duncan thought the same thang. Went one summer to Tupelo, Mississippi, at the mercy of Claudeen Draper, and lost

---

[33] Party or gathering amongst friends.
[34] Sexually promiscuous.
[35] To lack morals.
[36] Useless.

52

all she had. Wadn't two months and she came back broke,[37] bent[38] and battered." Mae drops her head.

"Ain't seen her since," says Rosalee. "When it was all over, she had to go live wit her Aunt Ida Faye, in Clayton." Rosalee shakes her head.

"…And that Willie Lampkin," she continues, "I don't trust 'em." She looks at Mae, on the door.

"Sumthin' bout his words and the way he talk. So full of shit, his eyes are brown."[39] Mae chuckles from the screen.

"I can spot 'em honey," says Rosalee. "A mile a minute.[40] Child, that man is slicker than snot on a glass door knob."[41] Mae continues laughing in the doorway, as Rosalee nods in the chair.

"Yep," says Rosalee, "sumthin' definitely rotten in Denmark."[42] Rosalee shakes her head in the seat.

---

[37] Financially unstable.
[38] Emotional.
[39] Con artist.
[40] Very quickly.
[41] Very slippery; a sly or untrustworthy person.
[42] A phrase from Shakespeare's *Hamlet*. Connotes an eerie situation or unusual circumstance. See Shakespeare, William. *Hamlet* (The New Folger Library Shakespeare). Simon & Schuster; New Folger Edition, 2003.

"Child," she continues, "I'm telling ya what God love: You better stay way from Claudeen Draper. And remember, that Willie Lampkin…" Rosalee pauses and looks back into the street.

"…Is bad news," she says.

Mae drops her head and returns back inside.

7

Later that evening Mae and Claudeen head out to Jessie's. While walking up the road, women and men are seen chatting about and provocatively huddled up. Fearful, Mae turns and whispers to Claudeen.

"Claudeen," she says. "I don't think this was a good idea."

"Girl, don't worry bout it," says Claudeen. "You here now and it's too late to go back home." Mae shrugs her shoulders and they approach the entrance.

Saxophones and raspy notes are heard from inside. A hairy gentleman greets Claudeen and Mae in the doorway.

"Claudeen Draper," he says. "Lord have mercy. Girl you killin' me tonight." Claudeen winks at him and inappropriately swipes his chest.

"You know it baby," she replies. Others whistle from the crowd and admire Claudine's curvy figure, from behind. Claudeen grabs Mae's hand and they proceed inside the club.

Inside, the atmosphere is heavy and rough. Claudeen, the true headliner, is seen waving to guests near the stage. Mae follows closely behind her. Claudeen scans the crowd, in search of Willie. But spotting Jessie, the club owner, she journeys over to the bar.

"Hey Jessie," says Claudeen. "Have you seen Willie? He said he would be here tonight?" Jessie leans over and whispers.

"Yeah girl, he's in the back. C'mon." Jessie directs Claudeen and Mae to the backroom.

As she opens the door, men are seen shooting craps[43] on the floor. Others are seen smoking cigarettes, drinking whiskey, counting money and carbon papers. Willie is seated on the edge of a table, with his foot propped on a chair. Cheap tobacco consumes the air. Claudeen and Mae watch, as Willie entertains the room.

"...And she says, Willie Lampkin, when you gone take me out? And I looked at her and said, baby you been out all night, just look down." The men roar in laughter.

---

[43] A gambling method, involving a pair of dice.

Willie looks up and notices the three women in the doorway and smiles.

"Well," he says. "If it isn't Claudeen Draper…" Claudeen bashfully smiles and looks off. Willie glances over to Mae Ruth.

"…And Mae Ruth Williams," he continues. He grabs Mae's hand and kisses it. But embarrassed, Mae rolls her eyes and quickly pulls away.

"You sweet-talk all your women like this?"[44] she questions. Willie grabs his chest, emulating a heart attack.

"Ouch," he calls. The room echoes with laughter. The sound of Jr. Walker seeps from inside the club. Willie lifts from the table and begins gyrating on a chair. Unamused, Mae rolls her eyes and moves to other side of the room. Willie glides to the door and calls from behind.

"C'mon ladies."

Outside, the club is clustered. Willie begins to flatter the crowd. As the band continues playing, he maneuvers through the sweaty pack and beckons for Mae. Edging closer and closer, he reaches out and grabs her hand.

---

[44] Flatter; pick up line.

"Dance with me," he calls. "Dance with me." But bashful and ashamed, Mae refuses. Willie continues his routine.

Claudeen nudges Mae on the shoulder.

"Gone," she says. "Gone and dance with him." Mae hands Claudeen her purse and joins Willie near the stage. The 45" remains in rotation.

Claudeen migrates to a back corner. In view, an unknown hand passes her a tube of a white powdery substance. The noise level soars inside the club.

Claudeen tilts the miniature cylinder, sniffing the substance off her hand. The room begins to twirl.

Mae cheerfully waves to Claudeen. Wiping her nose, Claudeen smiles back, as 440 Hertz fill the room.

The following morning, a rooster sounds outdoors. Exhausted, Mae raises in the bed. While sitting on the edge, taps are heard on the front door.

"I'm coming!" she snaps. "I'm coming." Grabbing her housecoat, Mae sprints to the door.

"Too early in the morning for this," she sounds. "Ain't nobody, but that cacklin' Claudeen." Mae swings open the door.

"Yes Claudeen!" she scolds.
But to her surprise, James greets her in the doorway. Tickled, she welcomes him in.

"Oh, hey James," she says. "You know, I thought you was Claudeen. You know she the only one, to wake you up at 7 o'clock in the morning." James skittishly giggles, as they walk into the kitchen.

"You hungry?" asks Mae.

"No ma'am," he responds. Mae twitches her lip, in unbelief.

"James, don't lie to me," she says. "I have more than enough food here."

Mae removes the bacon and biscuits, from the Frigidaire and heat them in the oven.

"I had plenty leftover from yesterday morning," she continues. "I always overcook and forget it's just me now." Smiling, Mae nostalgically looks out the kitchen window. James lowers his head, his eyes now watery.

Mae looks over, noting his somber face and quickly interjects.

59

"But," she says, "I'm glad you're here to keep me company." Mae reaches over and motherly hugs him.

Mae removes the food from the oven and sits it on the table. She journeys over to the cabinet for a plate.

"So," she continues, "what you doin' up this early?" Mae sits the plate on the table.

"I couldn't sleep," he says. "Nana been up all night, reading her bible and praying." James admires the food on the table.

"She said she don't like the things going on in town, and she don't like Willie Lampkin either." James takes a biscuit and begins eating. Mae looks out the window.

"Yeah," she sighs.

"She said this town was peaceful before he got here," continues James. "But now, since he been here, white folk been in and out of Sweet Lips."

Outdoors, much laughter is heard. Mae walks over to the front door. In the street, Claudeen Draper is heard arguing with Otis and Slim. Mae looks across the road, where Eva is seen kneeling in her garden and angrily mumbling.

Mae opens the door and goes out onto the porch. James snatches a piece of bacon, from the plate and follows her outdoors.

"I'm tellin' yall," says Slim. "Harold Lancaster told me them New York City boys make a fortune off runnin' numbers. Say the law and white folk don't even mine, long as they don't keep up no trouble."

"Yeah," laughs Otis, "and as long as they get they cut." Claudeen interrupts them.

"Boy, are you that dumb?" she says. "Jessie is the only one running numbers in this town and it's still done inside the club. Yea she do good, running the numbers, but she damn near done ran through her savings, tryna pay off the Sheriff!" Claudeen shakes her head.

"You gone and get your own number business," continues Claudeen. "And they gone find your ass dead, at the bottom of the river."

"Awl Claudeen," barks Otis. "There you go. Can't leave well enough alone.[45] Always makin' a mountain out of a mole hill[46] and blowin' thangs out of proportion. You ain't nothing but a dream killer." Annoyed, Claudeen fixes her hair.

---

[45] Disregard or ignore an issue.
[46] To make a great deal out of a situation.

61

"Otis, shut your liver lip ass up," she continues. "Ain't nobody killed his damn dream, but Willie. And just like I said, yall keep foolin' wit him and more than a dream gone come up dead."

In the midst of their heated discussion, Willie pulls up in his Cadillac and blows the horn.

"What's all the fuss?" says Willie. Slim admires the shiny car in the street.

"See Willie," begins Slim, "I told Claudeen that one day these numbers is gonna get me paid. Here soon, I'll be doing so good, I can start my own numbers business." Noticing Mae on the front porch, Willie rears back in the seat.

"…Yeah Slim," calls Willie from the car, "but you can't put all your eggs in one basket." Willie smirks at Mae.

"Numbers are good," he continues, "real good for business. But you gotta get somethin' nobody else's got." Willie looks over to Mae for validation.

"Ain't that right Mrs. Williams?" Eva raises from the garden and looks out into the street.

"Oh?" shouts Mae. "And I suppose you got the answer for that too, huh?" Willie raises up from the driver seat.

"Answer?" he says. "Baby I am the answer and best thing that happened to this town." Eva shakes her head in disgust.

Willie tips his hat and starts the engine. Slowly pulling off, he calls back from the window.

"Slim, you think about what I said." Winking, Willie looks over to Mae.

"And good day Mrs. Williams."

As Willie speeds off, Mr. Jenkins looks on, from the General Store, with great concern.

Slim and Otis are seen gambling in the street. Looking from her porch, Eva shakes her head in annoyance. Tossing money and throwing dice, Slim is noisily heard in the road.

"Yeah, let's go baby. Momma need some new bloomers[47] and daddy, a new pair of shoes."

Willie drives up, beside them, and dangles a bag from the car window. He steps out the car, removing several booklets from the bag. He places them on the ground.

---

[47] Feminine undergarments.

"What's that?" asks Slim. Willie cunningly smiles back.

"Pull tabs," he begins, "or as an old head once told me, Tips."[48] Willie roars in laughter, as Rosalee angrily watches from Mae's porch.

"It's sumthin' that'll get you paid," continues Willie.

The neighborhood children gather around and watch the charade. Willie observes the children, in the street and flashes a bright smile.

"And these right here," he continues, "these are your greatest customers." Willie beckons for the children and begins showing them how to play the game.

Mae opens the screen and joins Rosalee on the porch. Without hesitation, Rosalee turns to her and begins ranting.

"Look at him," says Rosalee. "Child, that Willie Lampkin ain't no good. I trust 'em about as much as I trusted Wilhelmina Shoemaker, with my

---

[48] An illegal gambling game. Booklets yield zero to multiple winners, with prize monies ranging up to $25,000. The person running the booklet, often known as the banker or the house, keeps a percentage of the money generated from the game. Some bankers charge $0.05 to $500 for participants to play. Many of these booklets are banned in various states.

purse last Sunday, when I left out to go pee." Rosalee shakes her head.

"But," says Rosalee, "if she planned on takin' sumthin', her ass had another thang coming. You gotta wake up early in the mornin' to shit me."[49] Rosalee pats her chest.

"It's always more than one way to skin a cat,[50]" she says. "And with folk like Wilhelmina and Willie, you always got to be prepared. The bible even say *be ye ready*,[51] and that's exactly what I was! That offering pan didn't get none of my money and Wilhelmina didn't neither." Rosalee rubs her chest.

"No suh,"[52] says Rosalee. "That bear wadn't gone dance.[53] I always put my money and blade in safe keeping."

Mae laughs from the chair, but Rosalee looks back into the street and rolls her eyes.

"He ain't got no shame," she continues. "Gamblin' and pullin' tickets wit the children. Next, he'll have 'em robbin' and stealin' from they mommas and daddys." Rosalee shakes her head.

---

[49] Trick or mislead.
[50] An alternative route to accomplishing a goal.
[51] Biblical reference to Matthew 24:44.
[52] Slang pronunciation for the term "Sir."
[53] A preventative measure.

65

"It just ain't right Mae Ruth, just ain't right."

Mae bows her head and sighs under her breath.

"Yeah," she mumbles.

But noting her response, Rosalee rears back in the chair.

"Yeah?" calls Rosalee. "Mae Ruth, don't tell me you sweet on[54] Willie Lampkin?" Mae shrugs her shoulders.

"Well," she begins, but Rosalee interjects.

"Well what?" questions Rosalee.

"Well," continues Mae, laughing. "We went out dancing the other night, at Jessie's and…" Rosalee interrupts her.

"…And," says Rosalee. "He still ain't no damn good." Rosalee looks out into the street and throws up her hands.

"Look at him," she says. Mae looks out, where Willie, Slim and Otis continue gambling.

"Look at him," continues Rosalee. "The way he stand. Just sorry, plain sorry. Child, my momma said you learn a lot about a man, from the way he walk. You know which ones are strong and goin' somewhere…"

---

[54] To like or romantically admire.

Rosalee pauses. Looking back out into the street, she points to Willie.

"…But the one's who ain't got no pep in they step…" Willie begins approaching the porch.

"…Ain't got no job," she continues, "and after your pocketbook[55] and draws.[56]"

Mae laughs uncontrollably from her chair, as Willie reaches the porch.

Upon his arrival, the women grow silent. Willie steps onto the porch and tips his hat.

"Ladies," he says.

Rosalee rolls her eyes, as Mae smiles back from the chair.

"Mae Ruth," he continues. "I been calling you and never get an answer." Mae blushes.

"Well, I've been busy…" she begins, but Rosalee interrupts her.

"BUSY!" blurts Rosalee. "With more important things. LEGAL things, especially a job." She looks deep into Willie's eyes. But humored, Willie sarcastically laughs back.

"Well," says Willie, "I'd love it, if tomorrow night…" He pauses and looks at Rosalee.

---

[55] Southern term for a woman's wallet or purse.
[56] Southern term for undergarments or panties.

"…If you're not TOO busy, to join me at Remington's." Resentful, Rosalee turns her head and shakes her knee on the porch.

"So, Mae Ruth," continues Willie, "I'll see you tomorrow night." Willie leaves the women on the porch.

"And good day Rosalee," he calls from the street.

Angered, Rosalee throws up her hands and continues rocking in the chair.

The following night, confusion is heard from Mae's living room.

"Hold still Mae Ruth, I'm almost done."

Kneeling in a chair, Silas Fleming attempts to hem the bottom of Mae's dress.

"You ain't never flinched this much," he says. Mae smiles and looks down at him from the chair.

"I know, I know," she replies. "It's just I ain't never had a man take me to something like this before, especially with a live band." Sy rolls his eyes.

"Child," he says. "What you talking bout? Jessies' got plenty of bands that come in and out that place, all the time." Mae blushes from above.

"Sy, I know," she continues. "But I ain't never seen one outside Sweet Lips." Sy looks up at her and shakes his head.

"Well," he says. "You just be careful with that Willie Lampkin, because the word is, he's bad news." Mae places her hands on her hips.

"You too huh?" she questions. But with distaste, Sy turns up his lips.

"Child," he continues, "I'm just saying. They say he gotta wife and six chillun[57] somewhere down in Alabama. And from what Marjorie Douglas say, he got a girl pregnant, down at her sister's church, in Summerville, Georgia. And she say he got another one on the way." Mae looks off and frowns.

Sy finishes hemming the dress and gives the seam a firm tug. Mae jumps down from the chair. She looks into the mirror and pauses. Looking down at the hem, she bursts with laughter. Sy bends his lips.

"Now Mae Ruth," he says, "what's the matter now?" Turning from the mirror, Mae giggles.

---

[57] Southern pronunciation for the word "children."

69

"Sy," she says. "Do you remember that Easter, you made that dress for me?" Sy rolls his eyes and bitterly replies back.

"Remember? Child, I'll never forget that day. Your momma never let me live it down. Every time I saw Henrietta, she reminded me of how I messed up that dress." He shakes his head.

"Honey," he continues, "I told Henrietta, I could fix it and to come back later on. But naw honey, she wadn't hearing it."

Sy looks over to Mae, who innocently smiles in the mirror. Gazing at the dress, Mae begins to think back.

1957

From the dream, Henrietta and young Mae exit the car and approach the porch. Sy opens the door and they proceed inside.

"Uh huh, honey," Henrietta begins. "I hope it's ready."

Sy walks into the living room and lifts a jacket and dress from the couch. But noting the miniature garments, Henrietta rears back, in much surprise.

"What the hell is that?" she questions. "And who am I suppose to put it on? A doll?" Intoxicated and slothful, Sy attempts to speak.

"Henrietta," he begins, "honey what you talkin' bout? That jacket is ready and the bust on the dress is fixed."

"You a bald-faced lie,[58]" says Henrietta, pointing. "I'm lookin' right at it. Sy, I gave you a damn pattern, the one layin' on that table and you did what you wanted to do."

"Honey," he continues, "that's a simplicity pattern, which means simple. I didn't need a pattern, I did it by sight. It'll fit. Mae put this on."

Sy hands Mae the garments and ushers her to the bathroom in the hall.

Pulling the dress over her head, Mae struggles to get inside. After a few moments of tussling, Henrietta calls to her from the living room.

"Mae!" shouts Henrietta. "Come on out here." Mae returns to the living room, barely inside the dress. Henrietta looks over to Sy and continues ranting.

"Look at it!" shouts Henrietta.

[58] To openly lie.

71

"Henrietta, just leave 'em," pleads Sy. "I'll fix it. Come back, later on, and it'll be fixed." Henrietta snatches up the pattern from the table.

"Mae," she continues, "go put your clothes back on." Henrietta turns back to Sy.

"I don't have time for this. Sy, I gave you this pattern, weeks ago. I don't have time to wait on you to fix something that shoulda already been altered. EASTER is tomorrow!"

Mae returns to living room, where Henrietta beckons for her at the door.

"Mae lets go," she calls. Henrietta turns around from the door and continues raving.

"Naw what you done, is painted yourself into a corner.[59] Yep, you bit off just a little bit more than you could chew.[60] You took on all them orders and knew damn well, they wouldn't be ready before Sunday." Henrietta motions from the door.

"But I know one thang," she continues, "this won't happen again."

Henrietta ushers Mae out the house and the two of them head for car.

---

[59] To over plan.
[60] Overloaded.

Silas looks on from the screen, as she slams the car door and speedily heads up the road.

A motor engine ruffles outside and Mae snaps back from the dream.

Looking out the window, she sees Willie parked in front of the house. With anxiety, she covers her mouth.

"Gone girl," calls Sy. "You look fine. Shitty sharp.[61]" As Mae exits the screen, Rosalee calls out from the other end of the porch.

"Yep Sy," says Rosalee. "Casket sharp to be exact and ready for the mortuary." Sy looks over to Rosalee and rolls his eyes. Mae turns around to Rosalee and raises her brow.

"Ain't you happy for me Rosalee?" she asks. Rosalee looks out at Willie in the street.

"Of course baby," she says. "Not everyday somebody from Sweet Lips goes dancing at Remington's."

Willie exits the car and walks over to open the passenger side door. Rosalee sternly looks at him from her chair.

---

[61] Well-dressed.

"…It's just some folk you can't be happy for or ABOUT!" Rosalee grimly eyes Willie, as he returns to the driver side. Rolling his eyes, he re-enters the car. Mae waves from the car window and they slowly drive up the road.

8

Slim is seen walking about the neighborhood, collecting numbers for Jessie. Sweeping the porch, Mr. Jenkins looks on in disappointment.

"Slim," he calls. "Why don't you turn them numbers loose and help me with the store?" Slim smirks to him from the street. Shuffling a wad of carbon papers, he looks up.

"Thanks Mr. Jenkins, but I rather work a job that's gone pay off." Mr. Jenkins shakes his head in disdain.

"Slim," he pleads. "Why not earn an honest wage? I'll even give you time off, to fix the cars with Otis." Slim continues counting the papers in the street.

"Awl Mr. Jenkins," he calls, "you just wait and see. I'mma start my own numbers business and be a businessman like Willie Lampkin." Mr. Jenkins' eyes widened.

"Son," he says. "That business you doin' with Willie, is only gonna lead to trouble. And Willie's gonna bring you down with him."

Nodding, Rosalee gives her input from Eva's porch.

"That's right Roy!" she yells. "Willie gone bring him down wit him." She turns to Eva, who sits beside her, picking greens.

"Lord have mercy," says Rosalee, pointing. "Will you look at that? Boy ain't been further than that rusty ass pole and Willie already got his ear.[62] I don't know why Roy keep wasting his time. It's like beatin' a dead horse.[63]" Eva shakes her head.

"I done sat here," says Rosalee, "over 50 years and seen 'em come and go. And he another one. Can't see the forest for the trees.[64] It's sad honey. A lost ball in high weeds.[65] Willie could lead him to hell and back[66] and he'd still be walkin' round with that silly ass grin on his face." Rosalee shakes her head.

---

[62] Attention.
[63] Pointless.
[64] Blind-sighted or ignorant to actual happenings or facts of life.
[65] Dumbfounded or misguided.
[66] A path to destruction.

76

"Probably got him on that reefer,"[67] she continues, "and doin' God only knows what else."

"But oh, when the cavalry come.[68] They gone have him and Willie's ass hogtied[69] or throwed up against a wall." Eva chuckles to herself and Rosalee nods in the chair.

"Honey," continues Rosalee, "shit don't run up hill.[70] And you mark my word, Willie Lampkin is shonuff up to something. He got more than numbers on his mind."

As Rosalee continues speaking, Slim reaches Mae's house. He calls to her from the street.

"Mrs. Mae, Mrs. Mae," he calls. "Are you gone play a number today?" No one responds.

Inside, arguing is heard. Slim remains silent in the road, but the noise elevates inside the house.

"I can't, that extra money is for the leak in the ceiling…Let go of me, let go…"

Confused, Slim looks over to Eva and Rosalee, who roll their eyes from the porch. Hesitant, Slim calls out again.

---

[67] Term for marijuana.
[68] Law enforcement or time of anguish.
[69] Earlier method used to tame pigs; notably used as a torture method against prisoners.
[70] Connotes a place of origin. References an original source.

"Mrs. Mae, you gone play a…"

The door abruptly swings open and Willie appears in the doorway. Startled, Slim attempts to speak.

"Oh…hey Willie," he says. "I didn't know you was here." Rosalee shouts back from Eva's porch.

"Me neither." Annoyed, Willie nods in sarcasm.

Slim nervously speaks from the road.

"Just trying to see if Mrs. Mae wanted to play a number?"

Mae appears in the doorway and quickly moves down the porch. Brushing past Willie, she rolls her eyes. In a loving tone, she greets Slim.

"Hey Slim," she replies.

"Hey Mrs. Mae," he says. "I was just tryna see if you wanted to play a number?" Mae angrily looks back at Willie and turns back to the street.

"Naw baby, not today. But thanks for comin' by."

Slim looks up at Willie, who fiercely mugs him from the door. Fearful, Slim turns and heads back up the road.

Mae looks across the street, where Eva and Rosalee are seen peering back at her. She drops her head and returns back inside.

Still in the doorway, Willie glares back across the street. Looking up, Eva shakes her head and continues picking her greens. Rosalee remains silent and sternly stares back. But smirking, Willie slams the door and walks back inside.

Later that evening, Mae awakes from a harsh nap. The room is hot and sweaty. Gathering her thoughts, she sits up in the bed. Now dusk, she looks out the window. Coarse notes ring from Jessie's, up the road.

Mae shakes her head and wipes the sweat from her face. She sleepily maneuvers around the bedroom. She looks down and notices the dresser drawers crooked from the hinges.

Remembering the insurance money, she withdrew earlier that morning, she becomes frantic. Gasping for breath, Mae begins tossing garments from the drawers. She looks under the bed and mattress, unable to locate the money.

Mae sits back on the edge of the bed. Tearing up, she stares at the wall. Still listening to the music from outside, she quickly jumps to her feet.

"WILLIE!" she exclaims. Mae swiftly dashes out the house, sprinting to Jessie's.

Outside the lounge, men are seen about the door. Women are provocatively dressed and flirting near the entrance.

Mae makes her way through the crowd. She enters the club, where she is greeted by Jessie, the club owner.

"Where is Willie," blurts Mae, "where is that son of a bitch?" Drunken and irritated, Jessie ignores her and continues drinking at the bar.

Mae abruptly breaks for the backroom. Putting down the drink, Jessie quickly follows behind her.

Mae bursts inside the room, where Willie is surrounded by women and entertaining men about a table.

"You son of a bitch," scolds Mae. "Where is my money?" Willie looks about the room and smiles.

"Ladies," he calls. "Will you excuse me please?" The women stand from their seats and prepare to exit the room. On their way out, they aggressively look back at Mae.

Willie remains seated and wickedly looks up. But in frustration, Mae grabs his shirt and continues ranting.

"Willie, where is my money?" she asks. "You know I was savin' that money for his education." The men swiftly intervene, quickly pulling her away.

Fixing his collar, Willie lifts from the chair and laughs.

"When are you gone learn Mae Ruth?" he asks. "He's dead, not coming back?" His words pierce.

Mae lunges for Willie, but he quickly grabs her by the wrists. As she struggles to break free, Willie fiercely shakes her by the hands.

"You need to learn," he continues. "I'm the best thing that happened to you. Hell, I'm the best thing that happened to this town!"

The men interject. They pull at Willie's arm, but he quickly yanks away.

"Shut up," says Willie. "Just shut up!"
Still gripping her arms, Willie shoves Mae near the door and slams down in a chair.

"Get her outta here!" he shouts. The men gently usher Mae from the room. Fixing the strap of her gown, Mae turns to leave. But halfway outside, she turns around and speaks.

"Willie," she says. "I'm through with you and you stay the hell away from my house!" The men look on in amazement. Shuffling a deck of playing cards, Willie viscously laughs back.

"You don't get it Mae Ruth," he says. "I own you and everybody in this town."

Shaken up, Mae angrily walks out the door, and the men quickly follow behind her.

Willie rears back in the chair and continues laughing, as the record draws to a close.

...Whoo hoo, whoo hoo, whooo...

9

The next morning, churchgoers fill the pews of Sweet Joy Baptist Church. The sanctuary is clammy and jammed to capacity.

Reverend Thomas steps to the podium and begins the sermon. Seated in the rear of the church, Mae occupies a pew near the window. Looking down at her sprung wrist, Mae reflects on the dispute between her and Willie, the night before. The preacher continues from the podium:

"…When you want better, you've got to go after it…"

Several minutes late, Claudeen Draper appears inside the church. Walking the main aisle, she scans the pews in search of Mae. Inappropriately dressed, Claudeen holds up her index finger[71] and continues her search. Walking back up the aisle, she spots Mae in the rear.

---

[71] A gesture known as "The Baptist Tip." It was routinely performed by slaves in church services; a signal to their masters that they were exiting, to use the bathroom. However, over time, the gesture became misconstrued. It is often interpreted as a form of apology, for one leaving in or out of worship service. It has also been used as an apologetic gesture for one's tardiness to service.

Claudeen enters the pew, crossing over several people, and noisily plops down beside Mae. Without hesitation, Claudeen leans over and begins to whisper.

"Mae," she says. "What happened with you and Willie last night? They talkin' bout it all over town."

Nodding and pretending to engage in the service, Mae bends down.

"It's nothing Claudeen," she says. "Me and Willie had an argument last night, at Jessie's. He grabbed my arm and when I tried to break away, I sprung my wrist." Mae looks up at the minister, who is still preaching from podium.

Dissatisfied, with her response, Claudeen loudly responds back.

"Grabbed you?" she barks.
At those words, people begin to look around. Now embarrassed, Mae smiles and aggressively speaks through her teeth.

"Shhhh Claudeen," she says. "It's nothin'. I threw him out. A little witch-hazel[72] and my hand will be fine!"

---

[72] Healing agent. Anesthetic.

Irritated, Claudeen sits back on the pew. She looks over to Mae and rolls her eyes.

"Uh huh," she mumbles and continues listening to the sermon.

Several men of the church are seen leaving in and out of service. Watching their movement, Mae begins to think back to 1957, a Sunday at Sweet Joy Baptist Church.

1957

From the dream, parishioners are seen waving fans. The minister is visibly sweating from the podium.

Eight year-old Mae Ruth is seated in between her parents. Antsy and agitated, she taps her mother on the shoulder.

"Momma, momma," she calls. "I gotta pee."
Henrietta looks down at her.

"Shhh, Mae Ruth," she says.

"But Momma," Mae continues. Henrietta bends down and whispers.

"Hush Mae Ruth! Hold it, service will be over in a minute." Disappointed, Mae looks around the room. Ahead, Deacon Smith is seen nodding off.[73]

---

[73] Falling asleep.

Further down her pew, Mae notices Clyde Nelson writing in his mother's bible. Now ready to pop, Mae nudges her mother once more.

"Momma," she begins. "I can't hold it. I gotta pee." Frustrated, Henrietta leans back for Mae to exit the pew.

"And hurry back," she says, as Mae crosses over her lap.

Mae creeps up the aisle. She looks up and sees Mother Wilson seated on the pew ahead. Mae continues walking the aisle and attempts to quickly pass by. But as she draws nearer, Mother Wilson grabs her by the arm. Terrified, Mae looks up.

"Child," says Mother Wilson, "where you going?" Trembling, Mae responds back.

"To the bathroom," she says. Mother Wilson shamefully looks down at her.

"NO you not," she says. "Now go back and sit down." Baffled, Mae walks back to her pew. She crosses over her mother and sits back in her seat.

Mae looks up at Henrietta, who is heavily engaged in the service. She turns around and looks back at Mother Wilson, who is gazing at the minister.

Ready to explode, Mae taps her mother on the shoulder.

"Momma," she says. "I gotta pee."

Now irritated, Henrietta sternly looks down at her.

"What," says Henrietta? "What was you doin' the whole time you was gone?" Mae twiddles her thumbs.

"I tried to go," she says, "but Mother Wilson told me to go back to my seat."

Annoyed, Henrietta looks back at Mother Wilson, whose eyes are fixated on the minister.

"Well," remarks Henrietta. "You go on back there and use the bathroom. And if Gerti has anythang else to say to you, you let me know." Mae nods her head in agreement. She exits the pew and heads back up the aisle.

Approaching Mother Wilson, her legs begin to buckle. Nearly passing by, Mother Wilson leans over and Mae comes to a halt.

"Girl," she says. "Where you going?" Frightened, Mae awkwardly responds back.

"My momma said I could go to the bathroom."

Mother Wilson looks over to Mae's pew, where Henrietta aggressively looks back at her. Mother Wilson looks back down at Mae.

"Well," she continues. "You do that and hurry on back."

Witnessing the entire sight, the ushers laugh and open the doors. Skipping out, Mae looks back at her mother, who continues watching Mother Wilson from the pew.

Mae snaps back from the dream. The preacher continues from the pulpit:

"If you want God to bless you, you got to be willin' to let some things go…."

The words linger.

The congregation stands to its feet. Somber, Mae glances out the window, where Willie is positioned and seen making drug transactions with several members of the church. Shocked, Mae looks on in disbelief.

Willie looks up to the window and notices Mae up above. He flashes a devious grin and arrogantly walks off.

10

From 1975-1981, Willie continues his drug operation, from inside the club. Slim and Otis have become his top runners and clientele soars for Jessie's. Patrons, journey for miles to purchase cocaine and gamble. Willie's relationship with Mae continues to spiral, often leading to full-fledged fights. He begins sleeping with Claudeen Draper, to pacify her drug addiction and manages a fiery romance, with Jessie, in efforts to continue his operation inside her club.

One evening, two white officers pull into Sweet Lips. Mr. Jenkins looks on from the store, as Rosalee stirs from her porch.

The men exit the patrol car and walk into Jessie's. All-knowing, Eva shakes her head in shame.

Within minutes, the officers surface and return to their car. The driver stuffs a thick envelope, into his pocket and climbs into the car.

As they quickly drive off, Rosalee chuckles from her porch.

"Tuh," she begins. "That Willie Lampkin even got the law[74] workin' for him. Payin' off the Sheriff and money launderin' with members of the church."

Eva's eyes widened, but Rosalee continues shouting from the porch.

"Honey," she says, "that man is far from a booger bear.[75] Naw child. That man, down at Jessie's, is the devil in a double breasted suit." Rosalee throws her hands, in exhaustion.

"Yessuh," she continues, "he goin' straight to hell, with gasoline draws on." Mr. Jenkins shakes his head and continues sweeping outside the store.

1983

After disappearing for a week, Willie returns to Sweet Lips. Heavily intoxicated, he is seen swerving on the road. Also drunk, Otis laughs from the passenger side.

Slim nervously looks on from the back seat.

"Yeah fellas," Willie begins. "I think this trip was a good one." He takes a sip from a flask. Otis

---

[74] Law enforcement or police.
[75] Loan shark.

erupts in laughter, as the car skids back and forth. But fearful, Slim interjects.

"Aye Willie," he shouts. "Man slow down. You gone get us killed." Willie continues drinking and yells back.

"Slim, shut up!" he shouts. "Just shut up. You know, Otis here takes it all like a champ. Good and bad." Waving his finger, he continues.

"You know what?" says Willie. "One or two things is gone happen, when we get back. Either your ass is gonna step up to the plate or Otis will become my number one runner."

Otis sobers up. But annoyed, Slim aggressively calls back.

"Aye man," he says. "You do whatever you have to do. But if you don't slow down, with all this whiskey, papers and dope back here, we'll never see the light of day."

Willie slams on brakes and swings around in his seat.

"I don't give a damn bout no law!" screams Willie. "I am the law. Hell, they on my payroll." Laughing, he lights a cigarette.

"What I'm scared of," he continues, "is shaky negroes like you." Willie nods and takes another sip from the flask.

"Yeah," says Willie, "you're my biggest problem. Too damn ambitious and it's gone cost me. You know what, get out." Stunned, Otis leans over and attempts to intervene.

"C'mon Willie," he pleads. "You can't leave 'em here. We're miles from the county."

Willie jumps out the car, forcefully pulling Slim from the back seat. Slim combatively exits.

"Aye man!" he exclaims. "What's your problem?" Otis gets out the car.

"Willie," says Otis, "you can't leave him out here like this. What if the clan is out here?" Willie flashes a scathing grin.

"Well good," he calls. "Maybe he can talk his way out of that one too. He always does." Willie gets back into the car and yells from the window.

"Otis lets go." Otis looks back at Slim and calls to Willie from the street.

"Willie," he says, "we can't leave him out here."

Looking out the front window, Willie yells back.

"Otis, I'm not gone tell you again. Let's go…You know what…" Willie reaches over and closes the passenger side door.

"…You can stay too," he says. "I'm done with the both of ya. Find your own damn way back."

Otis and Slim watch in disbelief, as Willie speeds off.

Later that night, Willie continues driving back to Sweet Lips. Drunken and swerving on the road, he mutters to himself.

"I don't need 'em," he says. "I did this. They wouldn't be nothing without me." As he continues up the road, flashing lights are seen in the rear view mirror. Hesitant, Willie pulls over. He attempts to gather himself and begins fixing his clothes.

Two white officers exit a patrol car and head over to the driver side. Chewing tobacco, the driving officer flashes a light in Willie's eye.

"Say boy," he calls. "You know what time it is?" Willie looks down at his bare forearm and arrogantly grins back.

"Can't say that I do?" he replies. Irritated, the other officer scolds back.

"Aye boy, you watch it."

The driving officer notices some duffle bags in the back seat. He signals to his partner, who goes over to retrieve them.

Inside the bags, the officer discovers drugs and carbon papers. Holding them up, he laughs.

"Aye Thomas," he says, "look at this." Noting the contents in the bag, Officer Thomas looks down at Willie.

"Aye boy," he says. "You mine telling me what that is?" Willie rears back in the seat and chuckles.

"C'mon fellas," he says. "There's enough to go around for everybody. Just talk to your boy Sherriff Hamrick. I'm sure he'll give you your cut." Officer Thomas smirks and shouts back to Officer Chambers.

"Aye Chambers," he replies. "I see we got us here an uppity one. Yeah, well we'll just have to teach this one here a lesson." Officer Chambers whistles in agreement.

Heavily laughing, Officer Thomas leans over, and hits Willie in the eye with the flash light. Noticing two more bags in the passenger seat, the officer reaches over to grab them.

Bloody and bruised, Willie moans from the driver side. The officers quickly return to the patrol car and speed up the road.

Dazed and woozy, Willie gazes at the fading road ahead.

The following morning, locals are seen about their porches and conversing in the street.

Claudeen passes through the crowd. Watching from the porch, Eva shakes her head. Claudeen looks over and rolls her eyes and walks over to Mae's.

Startled by the commotion outside, Mae retreats outside. Opening the screen, she is greeted by ever-meddling Claudeen.

"Hey Claudeen," says Mae Ruth. "Let me guess, you got the latest dirt?"[76] Claudeen clenches her chest.

"Mae Ruth," she begins. "Whatever do you mean?" In sarcasm, Mae looks off into the street.

"What's all the noise about?" she says.

---

[76] Gossip.

"You ain't heard?" questions Claudeen. "Everybody upset. They say Slim and Otis never picked up the numbers and ain't nobody seen 'em, since they left with Willie." Mae observes the grumbling bunch.

In the midst of their conversation, the crowd begins to cave in and screams are heard. In the distance, Otis is seen hopping in the road, as Slim straddles his shoulder.

Mae runs from the porch.

"What happen to you, what happened?" she commands. But sore and winded, Slim struggles to respond.

"We…we was heading back and Willie threw us out. He told us to walk home." Curse words fling from the crowd.

"That son of a bitch," chants an elderly man.

"He's ruinin' this town," yells a woman from her porch. "Sellin' dope and tearin' up folks homes." She peers over to Claudeen Draper. The atmosphere intensifies.

Mae travels over to console Slim.

"Did he do this to you?" she asks. Slim sleepily looks up to her.

"No," he replies. "I fell runnin' through the woods, near Pearson's Pointe. Didn't know if the clan was out, so me and Otis ran all night." Mr. Jenkins shakes his head from store.

A heavy-set woman[77] calls to Mae from the pack. Mae looks over and recognizes the harsh words spewing from Mrs. Jennings.

"Uh huh Mae Ruth," calls Mrs. Jennings. "So what you gone do now?" Stunned, Mae swiftly interjects.

"Now Evelyn," shouts Mae, "you wait a damn minute! I ain't perfect and I ain't tryna pin no roses on myself.[78] But ain't nobody finna hold my feet to the fire.[79] Willie is his own man and responsible for himself. I ain't seen or heard from him, in weeks. And I had nothing to do with what happened to them boys."

Watching the argument, Claudeen rudely interrupts.

"Now, how you like them apples?" begins Claudeen. "Mae Ruth ain't done nothing and truth be told, she ain't the problem." The crowd grows silent.

---

[77] Large or big.
[78] To wear a badge of honor.
[79] Pass judgment or publicly ridicule.

"Throwin' stones and livin' in a glass house,"[80] continues Claudeen. "Seem like you and yo husband got moe interest in Willie these days." Mrs. Jennings lashes out.

"Now Claudeen Draper," she begins, "you don't know what you talkin' bout." Claudeen smirks and calls back.

"Really?" she says. "All that money, Willie shelled out? For your house? After Mr. Jennings lost his job?"

Humiliated, Mr. Jennings studies the dry pavement below. But nodding, Claudeen continues.

"Yeah," she says. "You know damn well what I'm talkin' bout. And the rest of yall know too." The crowd begins to whisper, as Claudeen continues ranting. She turns around and addresses the clustered group.

"Uh huh," says Claudeen. "Majority of yall know that Willie been supportin' this town and the church too." Claudeen looks over to Reverend Thomas, who is seen nervously pacing in the street. Embarrassed, he quickly interrupts her.

---

[80] To pass judgment.

"Listen up everybody," he calls. "Listen up. Everybody just settle down and return home to your families." The crowd becomes combative and begins to shout.

Rosalee turns to Mae and shakes her head.

"Uh, uh, uh," she says. "It's sad. They done caught him with his draws down too.[81]"

Rosalee is interrupted by the sound of a car engine, rumbling in the distance. Shooting dust, the car abruptly stops behind the crowd. Willie jumps out and slams the door. In view, his appearance is muddled. His eye is severely swollen and his face badly bruised.

Willie charges the crowd, approaching Slim.

"You set me up," he calls. He reaches over, grabbing Slim by the neck. But despite his tight grip, the two begin to tussle.

Otis rushes over, tackling Willie to the ground.

"You sons of bitches set me up," yells Willie, from the dusty road.

"Let me go man, let me go," yells Otis. The townspeople look on in amazement.

"Willie!" yells Rosalee. "I don't give a rat's ass bout none of that you talking.[82] Now you barkin' up

---

[81] Exposed; caught.

the wrong damn tree.[83] If you know what's good for ya, you'll unass[84] that boy and let him go." Rosaelee pats her chest.

Willie ignores her and continues scuffling with Otis in the road.

"Set you up?" says Otis. "You put us out and we made it here, from the woods." The crowd continues shouting.

"Willie put him down," yells a husky gentleman from the furious troop. Shaking her fist, another woman scolds from the angry flock.

"Willie," she says. "Take your hands off him. That's a good boy."

Otis manages to break free, as Willie lays down on the rugged concrete. Willie looks up at the stout woman, hovering over him. He awkwardly stands to his feet and addresses the crowd.

"Good boy?" Willie says. "No ma'am, he's far from a good boy. And it's because of this boy, that my dope, money, and whiskey is gone." Whispering grows from the crowd.

---

[82] Unconcerned.
[83] To tread dangerous ground or overstep one's boundary.
[84] Release or let go.

"Chief Hamrick's boys," he continues, "got me last night. They beat me and took all my stuff."

Willie takes a flask from his coat, as cursing echoes from the crowd.

During the fiery ruckus, car engines roar up the road. Slowly rolling, they pull into town. Willie lowers the flask and looks out. Ahead, well-suited black men exit fine automobiles and maneuver through the pack.

Leading the furious band, strides a slender gentleman. With haste, he walks over and grabs Willie by the throat. The other gentlemen follow suite, joining in the brawl.

The crowd looks on in silence.

Soaked in blood, the gentleman bends down and pulls Willie by the collar.

"Don't you eva set foot in Harlem again," he says. The squat fella tosses Willie on the heated pavement and returns to his car. The other men follow and re-enter their vehicles.

Willie begins moaning from the ground.

"Help me," he cries. "Somebody help." The crowd begins to clear out. Crawling in the road, Willie continues begging.

"Somebody help me." Still sliding in the street, Willie angrily shouts out.

"Ain't nobody gone help me?" he says. Willie takes another sip from the flask and coarsely laughs from below.

"Yeah," he continues. "I made this town. You wouldn't be nothin' without me." The community looks on, as he continues raving.

"I put the steeple on that church," says Willie. "I did that." He beats his chest with pride.

Rev. Thomas beckons for churchgoers to return home.

"Naw see," says Willie. "He took out a second mortgage on the church, to feed his kids. And didn't make the payments." Willie crudely laughs from the ground.

"If wadn't for me," he continues, "yall wouldn't have nowhere to go let alone, talk about me or pray!" Willie reaches into his coat and lights a cigarette.

The crowd looks over to Reverend Thomas, who drops his head in shame.

Disgusted by the rant, Mae heads for home. But bruised and bloody, Willie struggles to stand up.

Stumbling on all sides, he guzzles down a few more swigs from the flask.

As Mae Ruth reaches her porch, preparing to walk inside, Willie calls to her from the street.

"Mae!" he screams. "Bring your ass back here. We got plenty to talk about." Sitting across the street, Eva begins rocking on her chair. James, on a step below, angrily watches the drunken act.

Willie stumbles up Mae's porch and begins shouting in the doorway.

James motions to leave the step, but Eva quickly grabs him by the arm.

"Mae," Willie continues. "Mae, get your ass out here." Mae surfaces in the doorway and shakes her head.

Angered, Willie grabs Mae's arm the two begin to tussle. For a moment, neither are visible and clashing is heard inside.

James stands to his feet, tentatively listening to the commotion. Screams are heard from inside the house.

The community surfaces back into the street. In view, Willie is seen crawling in the doorway. Bloody and weak, he moans from the porch.

Ruffled and drained, Mae stands before him, with a butcher knife to her side.

As Willie continues groveling on the porch, Mae lifts the knife, ready to stab him.

Eva gasps from her chair. But hearing her voice, Mae looks up. She looks out and observes the crowd shouting in the street.

"Willie get outta here," they yell. "Don't come back here." The chants ring.

"Get outta here. Don't come back here."

Mae drifts back to a tale, from 1946, when her uncle John Henry was banned from Biloxi, Mississippi.

1946-Biloxi, Mississippi

From the vision, John Henry is seen sprinting up the road. Sweating and carrying his knapsack, he runs up Dodgers Lane. Sheriff Finley and a few black farmers are seen chasing behind.

"John Henry," calls Sheriff Finley. "You stop right there. John, you stop right now or I'll shoot." But tired and panting, John Henry continues running up the lane. Lagging and out of breath, the Sheriff calls out again.

"Give it up John Henry. It's over." John Henry takes a deep breath and stops in the road. Moments later, Sheriff Finley meets him in the road, seconds before the angry mob ceases him. Standing before the crowd, Sheriff Finley waves his gun.

"Settle down," he calls. "Settle down." The crowd continues shouting.

"I'll kill 'em," calls a farmer, in the road. "He took my damn money. He slept wit my woman and ain't brought nothing but shame to this entire county. The man dives for John Henry, but Sheriff Finley quickly pushes him back.

"Quiet down now," says Sheriff Finley. "Quiet down." He turns to John Henry and looks him square in the face.

"John Henry," he says, "I want you to take three steps back and have a good look at Biloxi." John Henry's eyes widened, but Sheriff Finley continues speaking.

"You have brought nothing but shame to this community," he continues. "Your gambling debts, lies, deceit, and adulterous ways have caused nothing but strife in this town." John Henry observes the angry mob.

"These are good people," continues Sheriff Finley. "And everybody here has worked hard to make this town the very best." Sheriff Finley leans closer.

"As GOD is my witness," he says. "John Leroy Henry, if you ever set foot in Biloxi again, I'll personally see to it that you're hanged."

John Henry's eyes buck in amazement. He looks out at the townspeople, cursing him ahead. He quickly bends down, to retrieve his sack and begins to run up the lane. Sheriff Finley and the farmers look on, as he disappears in the sun.

Mae snaps back from the dream. Disoriented and exhausted, she looks down on the porch, where Willie is seen groaning for help.

Mae drops the knife. She looks over to Eva, who is seen clenching her chest. Mae turns and re-enters the house.

Mangled and weak, Willie manages to regain himself. He awkwardly stands and brushes himself off. Fixing his clothes and pointing, Willie speaks from the yard.

"That's ok," he sounds. "I'm done wit her anyway." Beating his chest, he takes another drink from the flask. Willie wipes his mouth, on his sleeve and throws his hand in the air.

"She couldn't handle me," he says. "I'll have me another one by tomorrow."

Willie stumbles into the road, nearly falling face forward. James looks up at Eva, who laughs uncontrollably from her chair. Watching from the store, Mr. Jenkins shakes his head in unbelief. From the street, Otis and Slim bursts with laughter.

Willie looks back at the townspeople. Throwing his hands, in defeat, he staggers up the road.

11

One week later, Sweet Lips experiences an unusual breeze.

Mae comes out, on the porch, to take in the morning air. Rocking in the chair, she observes the people of Sweet Lips. She looks across the yard and notices Rosalee napping on her porch.

Across the road, Mr. Jenkins is seen sweeping, as Elizabeth and Jimmy Lee Davenport are seen playing bare foot in the street. Ahead, Otis and Slim are busy fixing on Mrs. Baker's car, while Claudeen is heard arguing with Jessie in the street.

Mae looks out and notices the Motherboard walking up the road. Nearing her yard, they look up and roll their eyes.

Mae turns her attention to Louis Davenport, who is seen bickering with his wife on the porch.

"Woman," shouts Louis, "I know what the hell I'm doin'. I'm the one that put up the damn doe, anyway, and its fine."

"Louis," yells Juanita Davenport. "That damn doe bout as crooked as Fletcher Jackson, who came over here, tryna Jew me down,[85] wit that rotten ass meat." Juanita begins inspecting the hinges, from the door on the porch.

"You don't know what the hell you doin," she continues. "So dumb, you couldn't poe piss outta boot, wit the instructions wrote on the heel."[86] Juanita returns inside and slams the door.

"Awl hell," Louis shouts. "Just shut the hell up and gone back in the house."

Resting in a chair, Rosalee calls out to Mae from her porch.

"You know," she says, "it's a sad thang when a man ain't got no spine.[87] He rather live henpecked,[88] up under that woman, instead of goin' out and gettin' a job. Don't make no damn sense." With her eyes shut, Rosalee begins rocking in the chair.

Overhearing her, Louis lifts from his porch and heads for the road.

"Awl Rosalee," he calls. "Why don't you mind your own damn business?" Startled, Rosalee raises from the chair and calls to him from above.

---

[85] Form of bargaining. Stereotype about Jews in the market place.
[86] Intellectually challenged.
[87] To lack courage or zeal.
[88] Belittled by one's spouse or significant other.

"Why don't you tell your mammy[89] to mine hers and stay out my damn garden? Ain't nothin' but a bunch of thieves. Livin' off the system, while other folk round here strugglin' and raisin' your damn kids. You ain't nothin' but TRASH!"

Louis stares at her from the street. Embarrassed, he throws his hand and heads up the road to Jessie's. Mae smirks and continues watching, as Louis curses up the street. Rosalee lies back on the chair and angrily watches the sun come up.

Later that afternoon, Mae is seen napping on the porch. She drifts back to 1959, the day she met Lester Green.

1959

From the dream, Mae exits the house and runs down the porch. Henrietta calls to her from inside the house.

"Mae Ruth," yells Henrietta. "Don't go too far. Stay near the yard, you hear me?" Mae looks back at the screen and frowns.

"Yes ma'am," she mumbles.

---

[89] Stereotype and derogatory term for an African American mother.

Mae walks into the yard and begins twirling her dress. Up ahead, she notices Lester Green approaching the house. She quickly turns around and pretends to observe something on the porch. But irritated, Lester calls out to her from the street.

"Hey, Mae Ruth," he says. "I know you saw me." Lester wickedly grins in the street.

Hearing his voice, Henrietta lights a cigarette and watches from the kitchen window.

"Hey, do you ever leave that yard?" asks Lester. Mae swings around and stares back at him.

"Are you deaf or something?" he continues.

"No!" exclaims Mae. Lester budges closer to the yard.

"Oh, good," he says. "Well, let's go to Mr. Jenkins and get some candy." Mae looks back and notices Henrietta watching from the window.

"I can't," she replies. "My momma said I can't leave the yard." Lester laughs from the street.

"Mae Ruth," he says. "You never have no fun. Always up behind your momma."

The two are interrupted by the swing of Mae's front door. Startled, they look up and see Henrietta, dressed in a housecoat and standing in the screen.

"Mae," calls Henrietta. "What you doin?"

"Momma," says Mae. "Lester Green asked me if I wanted to get some candy, from Mr. Jenkins' store." Henrietta looks over to Lester and rolls her eyes.

"Uh huh," Henrietta continues. "Lester, how your aunt doin?" Lester nervously looks at her from the road.

"She doin' fine Mrs. Williams," he says.

"Uh huh," says Henrietta. Henrietta disappears from the screen and returns with her cigarette pouch. She removes a dollar and opens the door.

"Here Mae Ruth," calls Henrietta. "Come and get this money." Mae walks up the steps, to retrieve the dollar.

"Lester," continues Henrietta. "You got some money?" Lester looks down at the ground.

"Yes ma'am," he says.

"BOY!" yells Henrietta. "Stop lyin'. You ain't got no money and you know damn well I don't play no stealing." Henrietta digs back into the pouch and hands Mae another dollar.

"Here Mae," she continues. "Give this to him and don't be too long. I know how long it takes to get to Roy's and back." Mae skips down the steps, handing Lester the dollar.

Lester smiles at her and they head for the street. But noting the smile, Henrietta calls out from the door.

"And Lester," she begins. Lester turns around from the road.

"Yes ma'am?" he responds.

"You keep your damn hands to yourself, ok?" Lester smiles and nods from the street.

"Yes Mrs. Williams." Mae and Lester skip up the road, to the General Store.

As Mae and Lester near the store, they observe Barbara and Lucas Weaver arguing on the porch.

"Luke," calls Barbara. "You lyin' sack of shit.[90] I saw her. You and that damn Beverly McDaniel was at Jessie's."

"Woman," he says. "What the hell you talkin' bout? She said her alternator went out and I took her

---

90 A liar.

down to Jessie's, to use the phone." Barbara begins throwing Luke's clothes into the yard.

"Luke, you a lie," she continues. "You a damn lie. I saw ya and I want you out my damn house!" Barbara returns inside, to grab more clothing. Luke grabs the clothing, from the yard and put them in the car.

Lester pulls Mae, by the arm, and beckons for her on the side of Dale's barbershop.

"Lester!" exclaims Mae. "What are you doing? Momma said for you to keep your hands to yourself." Lester shakes his head.

"No, not like that," he replies. "I want to show you something." Lester removes a sheet from a wooden box.

"What's that?" calls Mae.

"Shhh," continues Lester. "Just look inside." Mae leans forward and notices a gun inside the box. Her eyes widen and she attempts to scream. But seeing her reaction, Lester quickly covers her mouth.

"Man, be quiet," he says. "You gone get us caught." Mae yanks away from him and moves from the box.

"Lester," she continues. "What are you doin'
with a gun?" Lester evokes a witty smile.

"I'mma shoot that fool," he says.
Mae remains silent and stares back at him. But sensing
fear, Lester chuckles and shakes his head.

"It ain't a real gun Mae Ruth," he says. "It's a
Red Ryder.[91] My cousin let me play wit it, until he come
back." Mae looks back into the box.

"Well," she says. "Why are you gonna shoot
him?" Lester nods his head and continues smiling.

"Because, that fool's always shakin' us down[92]
for money. Last week, me and Issac was walkin' back
from the club and Luke told Ike to hand over the
money, from the numbers. When Issac said no, Luke
punched him in the stomach." Lester bends down and
removes the gun from the box.

"And I'mma get that fool," he continues.

Lester peers around the shop and observes
Luke and Barbara still arguing on the porch. Barbara is
seen still throwing clothes from the banister.

"Get your shit and get away from my house,"
she yells.

---

[91] A popular 1950s style air bb gun manufactured by *Daisy*.
[92] To hassle or rob.

Lester crouches down and beckons for Mae below. He aims the BB gun in Luke's direction. Barbara returns inside and slams the door.

Luke goes to the car, to crank the engine, but the starter will not turn over.

"Damn!" he calls, hitting the steering wheel. He jumps out the car and pops the hood.

Lester repositions himself on the ground. He aims for Luke, who is leaning on the side of the hood. Lester lifts the gun and fires.

"Ping!"

Lester misses Luke, denting the driver-side door.

Lester looks on in bewilderment. He raises the gun and attempts to fire a second shot. But observing his trembling hands, Mae interferes.

"Let me do it," she calls. Lester looks back at her and rolls his eyes.

"What?" he says. "Can't no girl shoot a gun."

"Uh huh," responds Mae. She takes the gun from his hands and aims for Luke, who is still fumbling with the car engine. Steadily holding the handle, she places her finger on the trigger.

"Just shoot it!" yells Lester.

"Ok," snaps Mae. She grips the handle and closes her eyes.

"Pop!"

Mae fires the gun, also missing Luke and shatters the back of his car window. Lester's eyes buck.

Luke jumps from the hood.

"GOT!" he screams. "Woman done shot out my damn window. BARBARAAA!" Luke charges for the front door.

"Woman, I'mma kill ya!"

Lester and Mae run to the side of the barbershop. They look on, as Dale and the others, run out to see the commotion.

"MAE RUTH, MAE RUTHHHHHHH!" screams Henrietta, from her porch.

"Where are you?"

Mae jumps and sprints up the road.

Later that evening, Mae is still positioned, asleep in the chair. Rosalee walks over and joins her on the porch.

"Whew, calls Rosalee. "It's colder than a witch's tittie."[93] She sheepishly yawns and sits down in

---

[93] Very cold.

a chair. Mae skittishly laughs and attempts to sit up in her chair.

"Child," says Rosalee, smiling. "You ain't gotta get up. Always have been willin' and ready…Hmmm." Rosalee looks over to Mae in the chair.

"How you doin' Rosalee?" asks Mae. Rosalee begins rocking in her seat.

"Child," she says. "Feel like I been rode hard and hung up dry."[94] Mae laughs from her chair.

They are interrupted by a middle-aged white man, who pulls up to the house. Mae's eyes widened. The gentleman steps out the car and approaches the porch.

"Morning ladies," he says. Mae and Rosalee look at one another, with great concern.

"My name is Stephen Miller," he continues. "I'm from the city's Building and Development Department. I'm looking for Irene Jackson."

With suspicion, Rosalee professionally responds back.

"Well," she begins. "This here is Mae Ruth Williams and I'm Rosalee Harris and Irene Jackson

---

[94] Tired or exhausted.

doesn't live here." Mae cracks a smile, as the gentleman looks down at the clip board.

"Hmmm," he continues. "It says here that Irene Jackson lives at 8735 Dewberry Street?" In frustration, Rosalee rolls her eyes and looks over to Mae. She turns and points to the numbers on the house.

"This is 8733 Dewberry," she says. "Irene lives next door, but isn't home at the moment."

Reassured, the gentleman wipes the sweat from his brow.

"Ok thanks ladies," he continues. "I'll just leave my card and will you tell her I stopped by?" He pulls the card from his pocket and hands it to Mae. Rocking and nodding from the porch, Rosalee sarcastically replies back.

"Uh huh."

The gentleman re-enters the car and waves goodbye from the road. Mae leans forward, in her chair and begins to interrogate Rosalee.

"Rosalee," she says. "Whatchu think he wanted?" Smirking and surprised by her response, Rosalee places her hands on her hips.

"Child, you ain't know? Why, he's a modern day member of the welcomin' committee.[95]" Mae's eyes enlarge.

"Oh naw child," says Rosalee. "I'm ain't talkin' bout what they pulled in the 50s and 60s. Oh naw baby. Thangs ain't lily white,[96] no more and the white folk done took a different approach." She sits back in the chair.

"It's called gentrification," she continues. Mae frowns in confusion.

"Gentri what?" she asks. Rosalee shakes her head and chuckles.

"Gentri-fi-damn-cation," she says. Still confused, Mae stares back at her.

"Doris Crawford say it's somethin' new they startin," says Rosalee. "It's where developers come and offer money to poe folk, in exchange for they property. Years later, they rebuild the neighborhoods and fix 'em up real nice. And after all the black folk done took they little piece of change and ran, they sell back the land, to

---

[95] A neighborhood association, during the Civil Rights Movement, which strategically dissuaded African Americans and other minorities from moving into middle class and white suburban neighborhoods.

[96] A predominately white environment or neighborhood.

120

newcomers, at a higher price." Rosalee turns up her lips in disgust.

"Yep honey," she continues. "I guarantee ya, that's what he wanted." She looks back out into the street.

"It's sad," says Rosalee. "Folk round here strugglin' to get by. Tryna make the rent and feed a house full of children. Robbin' Peter to pay Paul."[97] Rosalee continues looking in the street.

"But honey," she continues. "It's some folk, who hurtin' so bad, that when the right one come along, they'll damn near hand over all they got or what they parents and grandparents done worked so hard to build." She observes the children playing in the street.

"Kids don't even got nowhere to play no more," she says. "Edward been done asked the city to repair the pipe, that's leakin' on Riley's field." She shakes her head.

"Children ain't got a safe place to play, let on be free."

Rosalee is interrupted, as Louis Davenport's youngest son and daughter run into her yard.

---

[97] Borrowing money to settle debts. Also references the earlier Churches of St. Paul and St. Peter, which bickered over taxes.

121

"Jimmy Lee," she yells. "You and Lizabeth just gone and get from round my yard. Runnin' round here like chickens with your heads cut off.[98]" The children ignore her and continue horse playing in the grass. Furious, Rosalee continues ranting.

"Children so damn hardheaded,"[99] she calls. "It's like talkin' to a brick wall."[100] She sits up in the chair.

"I tell you one thang," she barks, "yall break my flower pots and I'mma tear a knot so far in yall's asses, you won't know 'em from a whole in the ground."[101]

She leaps forward, pretending to come after them, but they quickly scatter into the street. Mae is overtaken with laughter, as Jimmy and Elizabeth Davenport mock Rosalee up the road.

"…Mae Ruth," Rosalee continues. "Have you ever been tied of the same ol' things? People won't raise they kids or somebody is tearin' up[102] somebody else's home." Mae nods in agreement.

---

[98] To run wild.
[99] Defiant or disobedient.
[100] Non-passage or non-comprehension.
[101] Southern term for a whipping or spanking.
[102] To commit adultery.

"You know," Rosalee resumes, "last night, Beatrice Eubanks cried in prayer meetin'. Say she think Claudeen Draper is sleepin' with her husband." Rosalee shakes her head in disgrace.

"Use to be a time," says Rosalee, "when children were seen and not heard.[103] Nowadays, that girl is seen and heard bout all over town."

As she continues speaking, Rosalee looks out and sees Claudeen fraternizing, with Susan Griffin's boys, in the road.

"Well I'll be damned," says Rosalee. "Speakin' of the devil.[104] There's the trollop now.[105]"

In view, Elroy and Tommy Griffin are seen conversing with Claudeen in the street.

"Child," Rosalee continues. "That Claudeen Draper ain't got no shame and don't care who it is. That girl a throw herself at a boy just weaned from the tittie, if you let her." Rosalee throws her hands in the air.

"And I hate to say it," she says, "but I'm glad my Joe is dead." In shock, Mae leans forward in her chair.

---

[103] Parental authority.
[104] Ironic or coincidence.
[105] A sexually promiscuous woman.

"ROSALEE!" she exclaims, but Rosalee continues raving from the porch.

"Honey," replies Rosalee, "ain't no need in bein' naïve. With a woman like Claudeen, round a man like Joe? Child, my marriage woulda ended before it really got started. It's pitiful, just pitiful." Rosalee looks back out into the street.

"Where are the morals?" she questions. "Years ago, there was good people in this town." She rests back on the chair and smiles.

"…People like your daddy," she says. "Now that Johnnie, child that was a very good man." She looks over to Mae.

"…A survivor too," she says. "Child, he could fall into a barrel of shit and come out smellin' like roses."[106] She nods in the chair.

"…And had a good hand.[107]" Rosalee points to Slim, who is seen conversing with Mr. Jenkins at the store.

"These young folk round here, think they know what gamblin' is? Child, Johnnie woulda put 'em to shame. He was so good at the craps,[108] he'd whip his

---

[106] To beat the odds; come out victorious.
[107] A successful gambling man.
[108] A dice game.

own ass twice a week."[109] Rosalee hits her knee and laughs out.

"Me and Henrietta couldn't wait till he got through," she continues. "By the end of the night, Johnnie be done cleaned house[110] and bought us all fish sandwiches when it was over."

"...And your momma..." Rosalee pauses and begins to cry.

"...She was sweet as pie. Would give you the shirt off her back." Rosalee wipes her eyes.

"I'd never forget," she continues, "when Raybon lost his job and him and Odessa was strugglin' to feed them kids. Child, yo momma would shoot over there, in a New York minute[111] and make sure they had sumthin' to eat." She continues nodding in the chair.

"Yep," says Rosalee. "That's the type of woman she was." Rosalee reaches over and pats Mae on the leg.

"Yep Mae Ruth," Rosalee continues, "you come from good stock.[112]"

Rosalee looks out and spots Linda Brown, coming up the road.

---

[109] A lucky hand or great gambler.
[110] Money won in a gambling match.
[111] To arrive quickly.
[112] Good genes or family values; an upbringing or rearing.

"Mornin' yall," says Linda.

Rosalee wittingly smiles and calls back.

"Mornin' Linda," she says. Linda waves, heading for the General Store and Rosalee shakes her head.

"Uh uh uh," she begins. "I ain't never seen nuttin' like it. Somebody that stingy. Woman stingy to her damn self. Tighter than a girdle on Sunday mornin.[113]" Rosalee frowns.

"Woman got money's mammy[114] and walk around wit her shoes run over like that. Sumthin' just ain't right." Mae smirks and shakes her head, but Rosalee continues raging.

"She gotta niece name Justine and she just like her. Used to come visit her durin' the summers. A low down,[115] dirty wench.[116] A real sass mouth.[117] Could get real jazzy wit ya."[118] Rosalee shakes her head.

"Sometimes we'd play together, but she was real foolish bout stuff and thangs. Real nosey.[119] Always

---

[113] A selfish or financially conscious person.
[114] Someone with substantial income or wealth.
[115] To be spiteful.
[116] An unsavory young woman. Common name for a prostitute.
[117] To speak sarcastically.
[118] Arrogant or disrespectful.
[119] Very curious.

mammy ridin'[120] and bulldozin' me,[121] bout where our clothes and furniture came from. And like I'd tell her, 'none of yo damn business.'" Rosalee chuckles.

"Mae Ruth," she continues, "my momma raised six girls, by herself. She worked hard for them rich white folk on that mountain. And everythang we had, the Good Lord blessed us with it."

Rosalee rolls her eyes and watches, as Linda rummages through a barrel of apples, outside the store.

"And a liarrrr," she continues. "Justine would lie bout anythang. I mean unnecessary thangs. Simple thangs. That girl would even lie bout what she ate for breakfast. And knew damn well, she ain't had no catfish at 8 o'clock in the mornin." Rosalee continues shaking her head.

"She even tried to lie on me. One time, she lied and said I wrote on the wall, in the Sunday school room. Yep, she sure did. And Linda believed her, because what Justine said was gold.[122] But, it just so happened it was bud nippin' season and I nipped[123] that thang in the bud.[124]" Mae laughs from her chair.

---

[120] Southern term for nagging.
[121] Badgering or pestering.
[122] To be accurate or precise.
[123] To settle or fix a situation.
[124] To address and put to rest a situation or circumstance.

"I told Mother Jones," continues Rosalee, "not only did Justine write on that wall, but her and Melvin Smith had been stealin' out the Sunday school money." Mae erupts in the chair, as Rosalee continues speaking from the porch.

"I'll learn ya durn ya,"[125] says Rosalee, giggling. "Linda was speechless, when they told her. You coulda heard a rat piss on cotton.[126] Not her niece. Stealin'? Child, she was done.[127] You coulda stuck a fork in her. She was so embarrassed, she moved her membership to a little old church, 10 miles south of Pearson's Pointe."

Rosalee nods her head and pauses. She looks back out into the street.

"But hey," she continues, "that's hither nor there.[128] And I ain't even mad at 'em. I've learned that people will lie on you, hurt you. Hell, they'll even dog you out.[129] But sometimes, just sometimes, you have to take it wit a grain of salt."[130] Mae smiles and drops her head.

---

[125] Teach a lesson.
[126] Connotes a still or quite atmosphere.
[127] At wits end.
[128] Irrelevant.
[129] To mistreat.
[130] Expect very little from the situation and move forward.

128

"Rosalee," she begins. "Where did I go wrong? Quincy left me and Q behind and Willie came and tried to take me for all I had." Rosalee looks over to her.

"Child," she begins. "Quincy was a man who wanted to support his family, but tried to, in a messed up system. I'm not sayin' his leavin' was right, but a broken man ain't much use to his self, let alone to a wife and child." Rosalee shakes her head in disappointment.

"Now that Willie," she continues. "I'm not one to say I told you so, but the moment I laid eyes on him, I knew he was no good. Big momma use to call it a spirit of discernment.[131] She use to say that sometime, they ain't even got to say a mumblin' word. But wit some folk, you just know." Rosalee continues rocking in the chair.

"Willie was just like my daddy," says Rosalee, "rotten to the bone.[132] No good in his insides." She nods her head.

"Honey," she continues. "Most folk like them already bad off, hurtin' deep down inside and wanna

---

[131] Within the Christian faith, a spiritual gift to discern and ascertain whether or not something is good or evil.
[132] Evil; bad.

put it off on somebody else." Mae drops her head, as Rosalee looks back into the street.

"I couldn't believe he was whoopin' on your head like that,"[133] she says. Tears trickle down Mae's face.

"Child," says Rosalee, "a man that don't respect you, damn show don't respect his momma. Hell, who knows, he probably beat[134] her out of money and in the head too." Mae remains silent, but Rosalee continues speaking.

"Baby," she says, "you gotta watch for the signs. I get so sick and tied of women saying he wadn't like that before. That's a damn lie. Momma use to say, if it walk like a duck and talk like one, it's a duck. Now I'm tellin' you, if he ain't got shit, ain't bout shit, and won't do shit, then nine times out of ten, he's full of shit." Mae laughs from her chair.

"I'm tellin' ya honey," continues Rosalee, "all the signs be there. And when you see 'em, you better damn run."

Mae bows her head and begins to chuckle. Surprised, Rosalee turns to her and frowns.

---

[133] Another term for beating or hitting.
[134] Steal; coax

130

"Now it ain't that funny honey," says Rosalee. "What's really got you all tickled?" Mae looks at her and smiles.

"You know," she begins, "we never talked about the night Willie picked me up for Remington's." Rosalee looks at her and shakes her head.

"Rosalee," continues Mae, "we never went to Remington's that night. Willie took me to some hole in the wall,[135] 20 miles outside Sweet Lips." Rosalee eyes buck.

"Well I'll be a monkey's damn uncle,"[136] she says. "Yall sholl had me fooled." Mae laughs from her chair.

"We wound up,"[137] continues Mae, "at some run down club that smelt like pee and the bathrooms didn't have stalls." Mae drops her head and laughs.

"And that ain't all," she says. "Now this gone grab ya.[138] Willie kept introducin' me to all these people. Somebody name Boogaloo, Boo Boo, Dirty Red and a woman name Dot Jean." Mae continues laughing from the porch, as Rosalee shakes her head.

---

[135] A deteriorating business establishment.
[136] Caught by surprise. Also references the Scopes Monkey Trial of 1925 in Dayton, Tennessee.
[137] To change course.
[138] To come as a surprise.

"I ain't surprised," says Rosalee. "It just keeps gettin' gooder and gooder." Rosalee turns to her and grabs her hand.

"Mae Ruth," she says, "we all got some stuff in our craw.[139] You gotta this and I gotta that. That's life baby." Rosalee edges forward in her chair.

"But child," she continues, "it's all a learning experience. And how you move on from it, will determine whether or not you learned something."

In the midst of their conversation, Hollywood is seen coming up the road. Mae and Rosalee look up and observe him from the porch. Laughing, Rosalee wipes away the remaining tears.

"Now that one right there," she says, "don't got all of what belongs to him,[140] or as momma use to say, crazy as a shit house rat!"[141] Rosalee laughs from her chair.

"Child," she continues, "Hollywood been crazy. Crazy as a Bessie bug."[142] Rosalee examines Hollywood in the street.

---

139 Imperfections and problems.
140 Mentally incapacitated.
141 A wild rodent that roams in an outhouse. Also references a mentally unstable person.
142 A chaotic person. Also references wild bugs in the woods.

"One time," she says, "your momma had just finished washin' her linens and come outside to hang 'em out front. Child, here come Hollywood, drunk as Cooter Brown[143] and naked." Rosalee turns to Mae.

"Child, Henrietta was madder than a wet hen.[144] She tried shooin' him off, but honey, Hollywood fell in them linens and that was it. Henrietta was fit to be tied.[145] You shoulda seen it. Him hangin' all out and her duckin' and dodgin'. Wadn't nuttin' between 'em, but the LORD and a smile."[146] Rosalee nods in the chair.

"Henrietta was beat red out the face. So mad, you coulda stuck a pin in her and she woulda bust wide open." Rosalee laughs on from the porch. She leans over and grabs Mae's hand and pauses.

"Mae," she says. "You got to forgive him." Mae looks over to Rosalee and begins to cry.

"Mae," continues Rosalee, "you got to forgive him. We wadn't there and only Quincy and The Good Lord know what happened that day. We know they was

---

[143] A tale about a town drunk; references someone heavily intoxicated.
[144] Highly upset.
[145] Term for exhaustion.
[146] Bear naked; possessing no undergarments.

133

near Hollywood's shack, but we don't even know if he did it." Rosalee takes a deep breath and sighs.

"Turn it loose and let it be," she says.

As Rosalee continues speaking on the porch, Hollywood comes stumbling up the road. He glances over to Mae and calls out.

"Hey Auntie," he says. "My name Hollywood and Momma name Sue Massengile."

As he continues speaking, Mae begins to heavily weep.

"Will you play with me sometime?" he continues.

With tears falling, Mae distraughtly replies back.

"I'd like that Hollywood," she says, "I'd like that very much."

Hollywood turns and heads back up the road. Rosalee grabs Mae's arm and they both continue crying.

Three days later, the sun beams over Sweet Lips. Eva and Rosalee are seen sitting on the porch, while James sharpens his knife, on a step below. Eva begins rocking in her chair, while Rosalee fans beside her.

Banging and hammering is heard from Mae's place. She surfaces on the porch and begins nailing the front windows shut.

Puzzled, James turns to Eva for clarity.

"Momma," he calls. "What's happening?" Rocking in her chair, Eva looks over and smiles.

"Change baby," she says. "Change." Tentatively watching, Mr. Jenkins smiles and looks on from the store.

Mae walks back into the house and returns with a large luggage. She drags it out the house and down the steps. Exhausted, she walks over to Eva's.

Upon arrival, she looks down and notices James' somber face.

"Aw now, cheer up," she says. She bends down and caresses his cheek.

"You can visit me anytime," she continues. James doesn't look up and Mae continues speaking. She struggles to hold the heavy suitcase.

"Well?" she says. "Ain't you gone walk me to the station?" James looks up, flashing a solemn smile.

"Yes ma'am," he replies.

He lifts from the porch and reaches for her luggage.

Mae turns to Eva and Rosalee, who are seen smiling above.

"Well," she says. "I guess I'll see yall later."

As Mae and James turn, to head up the road, Rosalee calls from the porch.

"Don't get too big in the big apple, you hear?" Chuckling, Mae responds back.

"Yes Rosalee, I hear ya," she says.

Rosalee lifts from the porch and continues shouting.

"And don't be walkin' alone at night."

Nearing the station, Mae turns around and yells back to her.

"Okk!"

As Rosalee continues calling from the porch, Eva lifts from her chair and places her hand over Rosalee's mouth. But, in hopes of getting the last word, Rosalee mumbles on.

Mae and James laugh on in the distance, as Mr. Jenkins continues smiling from the store.

12

Two weeks later, James goes to the mailbox to retrieve the mail. Inside the wad of papers, he sees a letter from New York City. With excitement, he attempts to open the envelope. But also anxious, Rosalee calls out to him, from Eva's porch.

"Hurry up boy," she yells. James beckons for Slim, Otis and Mr. Jenkins and they all huddle around the porch. He begins reading:

Dear Sweet Lips,

I'm finally in New York and you wouldn't believe how they treat you here. The train attendant was kind the whole ride and people from all over were nice the entire time. Now the meals, they were different from what we eat back in Sweet Lips. They served us somethin' called veal and asparagus. Now that sholl is a different kinda eatin', than what I'm use to.

Well, in spite of how Willie did me, with the insurance money and all, he didn't get everythang! Momma always said to have a nest egg[147] and I like to think, it's high time for mine to start hatchin'.

---

[147] Money put aside for the future.

To Otis and Slim, you've always been good with cars. My daddy's 'ol truck is just sittin' there, in that shed and I'm 900 miles away. So, you all can have it. Fix on it or take it apart. Sell it. But just don't stop helping people. Be an example for the community and show others what it means to be a decent person and good men.

To Mr. Jenkins, my second father. You were always concerned about me and Quincy Jr.'s well being. So, I thought it proper to leave my daddy's tool box. Since you're always fixin' and helping the families in Sweet Lips, with leaks and repairs, I know you'll put 'em to good use.

To Rosalee, my black Mother Theresa. Always giving advice and encouraging me to do better for myself. There's nothin' like humble words to a heavy heart. By now, I'm sure, you know I'm crying. So, I best carry on before my tears smudge the ink...You can have everything in my house. My furniture, momma's pots, the tea set, church hats and dresses. I know you loved momma, and I know she would want you to have them...

As James continues reading, he is interrupted by Claudeen Draper.

"What yall doin'?" she inquires. But anxious to hear the rest of the letter, Rosalee interjects.

"Shhh Claudeen," says Rosalee. "We can't hear."

Claudeen looks over to Rosalee and slowly rolls her eyes. She settles on the edge of Eva's porch and listens to the rest of the letter:

…And to Claudeen, I leave you my grandmomma's bible. May you find rest in God's arms and "only" His.

James stops reading. He looks over to Claudeen, as the others roar in laughter. Claudeen hops off the porch and storms off, up the road. James shakes his head in disbelief. He turns over the letter and continues reading:

…To Eva, I leave you my house. Your input has served as wisdom to my life. So many times, your unspoken words were my strength and have motivated me to push for more. Inside the envelope is the deed to my house. If you ever decide to sell it, you should get a pretty penny.[148] According to Rosalee, this land is worth a fortune!

…To James, my second son. I know pain still lingers at your door. But, I want you to know that what happened to Quincy, was not your fault and I never blamed you. God allows things to happen, in our lives, for many reasons and sometimes, it takes time for us to understand it all. Go over to Eva's porch and remove the bound envelope under her chair…

James looks at the others around the porch. They all look up at Eva, sitting in the chair. Eva raises

---

[148] Term for large amount.

from the seat and James removes the envelope, bound by string. Holding the envelope, he continues reading:

...Inside the envelope is a check for $5,000. After Quincy's death, I put aside the money for your education. I bound the money under Eva's chair for two reasons: 1) Because I knew that was the last place Willie would ever look and 2) I want you to do something great. Like the bound letter to the old chair, so is the golden connection we have to one another. Despite the pain we have faced in Sweet Lips, we overcame our past and now we push for a better tomorrow. Such acts of faith caused us to remain connected and reach down to find the last string of hope, moving towards a new day. And James, it is people like you, who remind me that, no matter how great the storm, brighter days are ahead!
Love always,
Mae Ruth Williams

James drops his head and the others remain silent. With her head bowed and eyes closed, Eva smiles from the porch.

Rosalee's eyes begin to water. Looking from side to side, she instantly jumps to her feet.

"Alright alright," she says. "Ain't no need in us gettin' all bent out of shape.[149] Piddlin' round [150] and

---

[149] To become upset.
[150] To waste time.

sittin' like knots on a log.[151] Cryin' ain't gone change nuttin'." She begins addressing everyone around the porch.

"We got to carry on, as Mae would want us to." She steps off the porch and into the street.

"Slim and Otis," she continues, "yall gone and get that car from the shed. You can use it to take some of the older folk round town." She turns and looks at Mr. Jenkins, who is smiling in the yard.

"Roy," she says, "you get Johnnie's tools and that tool box. Louise Burkett said her roof is leakin'."

Mr. Jenkins leaves the yard and walks over to retrieve the tool box. Rosalee turns around to Eva and James.

"And James," she says, "you get on down to the bank and deposit that check, cause you goin' to school!" She turns and looks at Eva, who is teary-eyed and still smiling from her chair.

"And as for me," she continues, "I'mma gone in there and get them pots and start cookin' for these kids round here. Cause God only knows the last time they had a decent meal." Rosalee proceeds across the street.

---

[151] To be idle or lazy.

Eva lifts from her chair and heads into the yard. Crouching on her knees, she begins picking greens and peas from her garden.

Rosalee turns around from the screen. Noticing Eva, now crotched in the muddy soil, she wipes her eyes and returns inside.

ABOUT THE AUTHOR

Dani Lou is a writer and native of Chattanooga, Tennessee. She is a graduate from the University of Tennessee-Chattanooga, where she earned a Bachelor of Science in Political Science and a Minor in English Writing. An avid listener of Mozart and James Brown, the author enjoys traveling and spending time with her family. She currently resides in Washington, D.C., where she attends Georgetown University. This is her first novel. For more information about the author, visit www.greentulippub.tumblr.com.